GW00537282

THE LAST PAYPHONE
ON
THE WEST COAST

The Last Payphone on the West Coast

a short story collection

by

Rich Perin

Buckman Publishing
Portland, Oregon

© 2019 Rich Perin

All rights reserved. This book or parts thereof may not be reproduced in any form, stored in any retrieval system, or transmitted in any form by any means—electronic, mechanical, photocopy, recording, or otherwise—without prior written permission of the publisher, except for the inclusion of brief quotations in a review.

 Buckman Publishing LLC
PO Box 14247
Portland OR 97293
buckmanpublishing.com

Last Payphone On The West Coast/ Rich Perin

ISBN: 978-1-7323910-4-8
Library of Congress Control Number: 2019901692

This is a work of fiction. Names, characters, places, and incidents either are the products of the author's imagination or are used fictitiously. Any resemblance to actual persons, living or dead, businesses, companies, events, or locales is entirely coincidental.

Book design by Emma Luthy.

"Trampo Marx in Space" previously appeared in Harpur Palate. "How to Boogie in New Orleans" previously appeared in Blue Stem. "Old Portland" and "Our Man in D.C." previously appeared in Buckman Journal.

Greetings from Portland, Oregon

Where I lead me, I will travel
Where I need me, I will call me
— Townes Van Zandt

TABLE OF CONTENTS

✳✳✳✳✳

OUR MAN IN DC
1

ROAD STEAK, THREE WAYS
13

NIAGARA AKIMBO
27

THE EXIT
39

THE BRIM OF LOS ANGELES
45

NEW YORK CITY
67

OLD PORTLAND
77

TRAMPO MARX LAUNCHES INTO SPACE
87

HOW TO BOOGIE IN NEW ORLEANS
101

OUR
MAN
IN
D.C.

Barron doesn't like his name. Never has. Doesn't feel any charm in its old world kitsch. He wants to change it but he's only ten. He tried abbreviating to Ron but his parents continued addressing him as Barron and most people follow the lead of his parents.

"Bah-*ron!*" The name sounds like a sheep swallowing its lower jaw, even when sung in a motherly voice. "Bah-*ron*, please don't forget to bring your violin to school with you today. And tell Maria to make pudding for you tonight. Not the rice pudding. The American one. Bah-*ron*, did you hear me? Come here and kiss mama before you leave."

Barron enters the dining room carrying his violin case. His mother is at the table eating scrambled egg whites with the latest issue of *Vogue Italy* open beside her plate. She dotingly inspects her son. He's in the midst of a growth spurt; feet and legs have stretched but the rest of the body is still waiting. She decided to let his blonde hair grow long and wavy so his head wouldn't appear small. "You are very handsome," she says and offers her make-up dusted cheek, on which Barron applies a dutiful kiss.

Barron is driven to school in a limousine. Along with the driver, there are two men with earpieces, one in the front passenger seat, the other riding in the back with Barron. They are not much for small talk. Not rude. They take their job very seriously, busy surveying all the angles, avoiding distraction.

The limousine stops at the gated driveway of the school. The earpiece man in the front seat gets out and nods at the Vice Principal who is busy ushering arriving children. Earpiece man in the back exits and holds the car door open for Barron. Vice Principal cheerfully booms, "Good morning, master Barron!"

"Good morning, Mr..." and before Barron can complete the greeting, the Vice Principal is booming another welcome at the next student. The limousine drives away, leaving the earpiece men standing guard at the school's gate.

Barron walks up the elm-lined causeway that parades through the school's fertilizer drunk lawns and flower beds. It ends at a stack of Olympian steps, where students mill, waiting for the bell. The school building is from the 19th century, a regal two story red brick, with ivy twined on its walls. Above giant oak doors, stained glass windows featuring solemn saints sanctifying the entrance. Barron enters and steps into the foyer. The school smells like furniture polish and tweed coats. Barron walks down the center corridor, through maddening classmates of Elspeths, Willows, Spencers, Percivals, who are preparing for class, gossiping, and like generations before, leaning against the wood paneling, rubbing them to a sheen. Barron slaloms through, past his locker, past classrooms, bathrooms, janitorial closets, to the back doors of the building that mirror the front, opens them and exits.

He keeps walking, along another causeway parading through more lawn and flowers. The school bell rings as Barron strolls by the sporting field. He reaches a parking lot, where Mr. Nosh, driving his dented two-door hatchback, screeches in, parks, and runs past Barron with a trail of loose paperwork flapping after. A wall announces the end of the school grounds. Barron throws his violin case over and climbs the wall.

The other side is what it was like before development. Tall weeds. Decaying plant-life under new verdant. Plentiful insects winging constant buzz. Then a ragged forest, a few tall trees with Spanish moss roosting in its crevices, but mostly a dense array of smaller trees and bramble bush.

Barron continues walking, crunching twigs and dead leaves underneath, interrupting spider webs, venturing deeper. Five minutes into his trek the earth gets softer. He sees a river and heads towards it but the ground progressively loses firmness and turns to porridge that sucks at his shoes with each step. Walking downstream scouting for drier ground, Barron spots a small clearing fifty yards inland. In it, a worn brown tent is pitched with a tarp strung above it. There is activity at the camp. Barron creeps closer, sees a woman sitting beside a five-gallon bucket scrubbing and rinsing clothes. With her is a shirtless man throwing a pocket knife into the trunk of a fallen tree. The sound of the knife in flight, followed by the *thwick* of the blade stabbing into the wood, is more impressive than any video game Barron has played.

"I'm just saying, woman," says the shirtless man while pulling the knife from the log, "that there's a whole river just over there and I can bring you a bucket of that instead of drinking water."

"Pfft! That water's got algae and road spill," says the woman. She finishes wringing a shirt, glances up, and sees Barron watching. "Jay-sus! Where did you come from!"

"Hello," says Barron. "I didn't mean to scare you."

"You gave me a good fright," says the woman. She flutters a hand over her chest to help catch her breath. "I wasn't expecting anyone."

"Are you lost, bud?" asks the shirtless man.

"No," says Barron.

The woman notices Barron's uniform. "You're from that school back there, ain't ya?"

Barron nods.

The shirtless man throws the knife into the log. His tan is deep from years of uninterrupted sun. A large scar crescents pink on a shoulder blade. Long hippie hair, the salt almost entirely banishing the pepper, falls down his back. "Woo-ee! You're playing hooky. Well, come on in, you're one of our kind. You wanna Coke?"

"Sure," says Barron and he walks into the camp.

The shirtless man unzips the tent, crawls halfway in and comes out with a can of Coke. "Don't have ice but it's cool enough," he says giving the can to Barron.

"Thank you."

"My name is Mitch," says shirtless. "And that there is Oleanda."

Oleanda finishes hanging clothes on tree branches and through her hive of let-loose hair she smiles a hello. One of her front teeth is vastly overcrowding the other. "That's Oleanda with an 'a' at the end," she says.

"That's a pretty name," says Barron.

"Ha! You're just a heart breaker," chuckles Oleanda. She's petite and jaundiced, a decade or two younger than Mitch. Acne shames her face. "I like your hair," she says. "What's your name?"

"Ray Ray," says Barron.

Mitch laughs. "Well, shit, pleased to make your acquaintance, Ray Ray." Mitch sits on the log and points to a stump. "Take a load off. Tell us of your travels."

Barron takes off his backpack and sets down his violin case. "I just walked away from school, that's all," he says as he sits. "Do you live here?"

"For the time being, yes," answers Mitch.

"Aren't you bothered by the cockroaches and millipedes?"

"I admit they take a little to get used to but there's good bugs, too, like fireflies. Pockets of the forest glow like Christmas trees, so bright that Oleanda reads her Harry Potters by their light."

"Really?"

"Yes, indeed. You can't dismiss bugs. They have a right to live here as much as any other living thing. It's like riding public transport. We're all neighbors."

Barron pauses, his eyes looking away at nothing in particular, politely giving the appearance of consideration. Then he asks, "Why were you throwing the knife into the log?"

"I was practicing mumblety-peg," says Mitch.

"Huh? Mom's nutmeg?"

"Mumblety-peg. It's a game of skill down south used to settle disputes."

"My father travels to the south a lot," says Barron. "Florida. To play golf."

"I'm not a golf man, myself. Fine game, I hear, though." Mitch unsticks the knife from the log and hands it to Barron. "The idea of mumblety-peg..."

"Don't teach the boy that stupid game," interrupts Oleanda.

"We're not gonna play it," retorts Mitch. "Just explaining the rules. The art and craft. Can't deny a young mind culture, you know."

Barron notices the weight of the pocket knife. It's heavier than the cutlery he uses for dinner. The blade sharply defiant. Barron admires the handle. It's like wood. And carved into it is a fish, finely detailed with gills, scales, and tail.

"That's caribou bone," says Mitch. "My great-granddaddy won this knife in a Faro game during the Yukon gold rush."

Oleanda smiles at the remark.

Barron folds the blade back into the caribou handle. Then opens the blade again. Mitch prompts its return and Barron hands it back.

Mitch stands. "In mumblety-peg, the adversaries face each other, about a body length apart, in a relaxed stance where the feet line up with shoulders. Like this." Mitch settles his feet back and forth like a cat kneading its paws, crouches a little forward, arms perched at his side as if he is about to quick draw. "Once the opponents are set, they count down in unison. Three. Two. One. And they throw their knife into the ground as close as possible to their own foot. The closest wins." Mitch flicks the knife; it stabs the ground two inches away from his left foot. The blade wants to plunge further but the handle impedes its insistence.

Barron is exhilarated by the dare. "What happens if you stab your own foot?" he asks.

"You automatically win. Hurts plenty, though." Mitch looks like he's recounting a memory. "Oooh-ieee! Hurts like a bitc... I mean it hurts a lot."

"What if the other guy stabs his own foot, too?"

"Then you have a pair of fools and everyone should back out slowly."

"I don't know if I'd be any good at it," says Barron.

"You don't play mumblety-peg unless you have years of knife skills and familiarized yourself with your blade," warns Mitch. "Each knife weighs differently. A different sense of balance. It takes time to learn it. You just don't willy nilly into a mumblety-peg match."

Barron nods. "Can I throw the knife into the log?"

"Sure." And Mitch instructs how to throw the knife, not all wrist and not all arm but a balance between the two. Barron's first throw hits the bottom of the log and the knife flops flat onto the dirt.

Mitch retrieves the knife and returns it to Barron. "Now you try that again, Ray Ray, and give it a little more wrist." And this time the knife spins through the air and sticks in the log with a proud *thwick*. "That's it!" encourages Mitch. "You getting it now."

As the boys practice their knife throws, Oleanda sits next to Barron's violin case and runs a finger across it. She unlatches and slowly opens the case. "This sure is a pretty fiddle," says Oleanda.

Barron is more keen with the knife. "I guess so."

"I used to play fiddle all through school," says Oleanda.

"You mind if my Olive plays some?" asks Mitch. "She's real good at it."

"Sure," says Barron, "but it's probably out of tune."

Oleanda picks it up and plucks the strings. She collects her hair and ties a ponytail. Composed, she tucks the violin to her neck and tunes it. Then a scale timidly squeaks out. Soon, though, her fingers remember and her command is apparent. She plays a mountain folk song that gains pace. Oleanda with bad skin looks good with a violin under her chin.

"Goddamn, gal!" Mitch hoots. He starts dancing, his feet tap precise and snappy but his strides wide and goofy like a clog dancer. Above his mid-riff he remains stiff and upright, thumbs hooked on belt, sometimes unhooked to slap his thighs, accenting the upbeat.

Barron has never heard his violin so right. He unbuttons his shirt, removes it, and starts dancing. His lanky form wiggles asymmetrical, movement disjointed but oddly syncopates to the rhythm.

They do this for some time and build up a sweat. Then Mitch calls for a smoke break and rolls himself a cigarette.

"Mitch was going to grill up some hot dogs that need to get eat today," says Oleanda. "You're welcome to join us. We don't have any bread but we got tortillas and ketchup."

Barron accepts.

After lunch, Oleanda notices the mud on Barron's pants, especially around the ankles, and insists on cleaning them. "Otherwise," she says, "you'll draw suspicion and get busted." As the pants dry, Mitch and Barron practice throwing the knife. Mitch recounts he once owned a taxi and how one night, years back, he swears to God, that Bill Clinton and Monica Lewinsky made love in the back of his cab. Barron doesn't know who Monica Lewinsky is.

The day starts to reach its warmest. "I should go back

to school," says Barron. "They'll be getting out soon and my ride will be waiting."

"Too true, too true," says Mitch. "Well, I can't say how long me and Oleanda will be camped out here but if you come back this way, be sure to check up."

Barron nods.

"And instead of going back the way you came, go inland this way," directs Mitch, "and you'll hit a little gravel road that will take you to the school. You don't want to get your pants all muddy again."

Mitch clamps a solid handshake. Oleanda warmly hugs. Barron departs through the thicket.

The trees and bramble quickly conceal the camp. After walking for five minutes, a gravel road appears, barely breaking the overgrowth. Barron is walking down it when he hears Oleanda calling in the distance. "Ray Ray! Hey, Ray Ray!" she yells. "You forgot your fiddle!" Barron picks up his pace then starts running towards the school.

ROAD STEAK, THREE WAYS

Truck Stop Microwave and Engine Oven

Jerome Johnson is eating a steak sandwich, a bloody affair between two slices of disintegrating Wonder Bread. The steak, a bacon-wrapped filet mignon, was somewhat cooked in the microwave of a truck-stop gas station. Jerome is enjoying his meal in the passenger seat of a minivan that's cruising the slow lane of an interstate. With fats and cow juice glistening his chin's stubble, he speaks. "It's a little rare. Could use an extra minute. I programmed it for 7 on medium-high but I saw the old gal behind the counter didn't like us messing with her microwave." Jerome grimaces while taking another bite then offers the sandwich to the driver. "Here, have some now. I'm gonna souse it up with heat." Cradled between his legs is a Slurpee cup filled with individual packets of hot sauce. In the state penitentiary, five hot sauces are worth a factory rolled cigarette. They are known as fifths.

Driving the minivan is Rodrigo Cardenas, a wiry, but strong, young man with an earnest goatee dashing his chin.

He's coming back from Alaska, the mouth of the Egigek River, where he was second mate in a three-crew skiff that trolled sockeye salmon. His job involved casting nets, pulling them in, untangling the sockeye, and bleeding them. It paid plenty, but considering the long hours sloshing in fish guts, the persistent daylight, and the constant creep of cold, Rodrigo felt it should have been more. Still, 11 thousand cash is a handsome bundle. He took 54 of the Ben Franklins, like a deck of cards with jokers, and made a flip-book animation with the stack. Nothing spectacular – just a fish swimming from one corner to the other, dodging a net. This stack he will not divide, not until he is back home in Texas. The idea of showing the earnings to his mother and sisters fills him with pride. He has never been away from them for months at a time. Nor at such a distance. Still, Rodrigo Cardenas doesn't think he'll stay in Texas for long. He has a new appreciation for firm ground under his feet and wants to explore the surety further afield.

Rodrigo declines the steak sandwich. "In an hour, my burrito will be ready," and nods his head to the front of the peeling-paint minivan. He is talking about the burritos wrapped in foil, wedged beside the engine block. "Next time let me heat the burritos first," says Rodrigo. "You can't microwave frozen burritos and steak at the same time."

Jerome looks over his left shoulder. Holding up his sandwich, chewing half-cooked bacon, he says, "Whattabou' you, Aziz?"

Aziz Mossaddegh sits behind on the middle row bench seat. He is wearing mirrored sunglasses, a soccer jersey, shorts, and unblemished Nike sneakers with white ankle socks. A stylish salon haircut crests his head. His handsome olive-toned face is smooth and fresh, the chore of shaving not yet a regular habit. He is gnawing on peppered elk jerky. "I will eat this while my burrito cooks," he says in a thick German accent. "I never have eaten elk. It is very tough. Like shoes."

Jerome returns facing forward. "If given enough time, yes sir, a microwave can cook a piglet with a burrito in its mouth. Positioning is important. You gotta know where the hot-spots are." He swallows and continues. "Microwaves sure are sensitive. Like women. You gotta bond with 'em before you can cook a decent meal. Must not be rushed. When things are rushed that's when expectations don't match results."

The Acquisition

Rodrigo pinned a note on the message board at the Seattle backpacker hostel offering a ride to Texas in exchange for gas money. Jerome responded within an hour, needing to get to Houston by the end of the month. Aziz was a late addition, discovering the note the morning of departure and quickly deciding a road trip to Austin was far more comfortable than a Greyhound bus. After driving across Washington, it is clear that the three personalities are not too much at odds.

In Chubbuck, Idaho, while Rodrigo and Aziz are in an auto parts store buying windshield wipers, Jerome notices a delivery truck at the back door of a nearby diner. When the truck leaves, Jerome exits the minivan and tests his luck at the diner's service entrance, discovers it unlocked, and snatches two boxes from the recent delivery. One contains 18 frozen filet mignons, the other packets of hot sauce.

Rodrigo and Aziz return to find an empty van. "Where

do you think that odd chap is?" asks Aziz.

Rodrigo lifts the van's hood and uncaps the wiper fluid reservoir. "Say what?"

"Jerome. I think he is an odd fellow. Wouldn't you say? Where do you think he is?"

Rodrigo shrugs his shoulders and pours.

"In that case," announces Aziz, "I am going to sit in the front seat." He opens the door and settles himself inside.

Rodrigo hears rustling from a hedge at the end of the parking lot. A raspy whisper comes from it. "Rodrigo! Hey! Rodrigo!"

Rodrigo turns around and sees Jerome kneeling behind the hedge. "Uh, what are you doing, man?" he asks.

"Act cool. Act cool. Go back to the engine."

Rodrigo returns to the reservoir. "Ok. What's happening?" he asks, hoping the calm of his voice settles the jittery Jerome.

"Just hurry up and finish, but don't act too fast." Forgetting that Rodrigo has his back turned, Jerome gestures to his left. He is too busy keeping an eye on the diner's delivery door. "Meet me around the corner."

"Which corner?"

Jerome points again. "That one."

"What?"

"Over there!" he hisses.

Rodrigo drops his request for clarification. With only two options at the parking lot exit, it doesn't really matter. Finishing the refill, Rodrigo lowers the hood, replaces the wipers, then gets into the driver's seat and starts the minivan.

"We are leaving Jerome?" asks Aziz.

"No. He was hiding in the bushes and says to meet us around the corner."

Aziz's eyebrows furrow into perplexity. "This makes no sense."

At the parking lot exit, they spot Jerome waiting a block away with two boxes gorilla-held under his arms.

Rodrigo pulls up. The side door shoots open, boxes fly in, followed by a diving Jerome. "Go! Go! Go!" yells Jerome. Within sixty seconds, they are on the highway, closing in on the county line.

Hobo Rotisserie

It's a night where the sky has nothing to hide, the full extent of the Milky Way's spill exposed. The moon is low and thin. No clouds, no city lights, no trees, mountains far in the distance more like a ripple than interruption, just the universal yaw belittling everything beneath. Jerome feels it acutely, but is telling himself to enjoy the immensity.

It's a side-out of a state highway in Utah. Sitting in camping chairs, Jerome, Rodrigo, and Aziz each hold a stick spiked with a bacon-wrapped filet mignon. They are hanging their steaks over a makeshift campfire. Jerome has an extra steak stabbed on his hobo rotisserie.

Fat drips into the fire and spits. The fire illuminates a dozen feet, beyond that only shapes with faded outlines, the darkness of the night makes further definition a gamble.

"Man, are those stars always out there like that?" questions Jerome. "I've never seen anything like it in real life."

"Careful, man, your bacon is slippin'," says Rodrigo, pointing at Jerome's steaks.

"You have to rotate the steak constantly, in an even manner," offers Aziz. "Otherwise that will happen, yes?"

Jerome's bacon catches fire, transforming his stick into a torch. He waves it around, the swooshing gathers more oxygen, the combustion intensifies, until the steak flies off the stick like a flaming bale set forth from a catapult, over his shoulder, and onto the highway where it lays sizzling, a fat fueled flare, spluttering into expiration.

"Shieet," says Jerome. He returns his remaining impaled steak over the fire. This time he's more focused and rotates carefully. "Man, I hate wasting meat like that. I was without steak for eight years, goddammit. These surroundings spook me. Too big. Bigger than big. I don't know. It's unsettling."

"I thought you'd love it," says Rodrigo. "You know, wide open spaces. No walls or razor wire."

"I enjoy it when we're on the road, but at night, not moving, everything is far away. Makes me feel small."

"Maybe this will help," and Rodrigo removes a joint from his shirt pocket and passes it to Jerome. "Wings, my friend."

"My brother!" Jerome gives the joint a connoisseur sniff. "How the hell did you slip this by the po-leece?"

"They let the dog loose on the inside but nowhere near the master brake cylinder."

"Crafty!"

"This is good news!" proclaims Aziz.

Earlier, in Idaho, they were idle for several hours on the shoulder of a freeway, sequestered at the pleasure of the state highway patrol. Their names were run through warrant databases, Aziz's student visa doubled-checked with the Department of Homeland Security. One of the state troopers was bemused, repeating "Huh, a *German* A-rab" and "*German* Mu-slim" several times. Aziz thought it appropriate to correct the state trooper, declaring that he wasn't a Muslim but rather an atheist, and of Persian descent. The officer responded by calling headquarters and requesting the dog squad for a vehicle search. The K-9 unit arrived an hour later. It was a new dog. It searched over-enthusiastically, tearing bags, eating half a loaf of Wonder Bread, chewing a head rest, and, after having its fun, the dog sat proudly outside the van unable to report any contraband. The state troopers didn't apologize for the dog's ruin. Instead, Rodrigo was issued a ticket for distracted driving. The ticketing trooper also pointed out that the minivan needed new windshield wipers but wouldn't issue a citation if Rodrigo promised to stop at the next town and purchase new ones. The trooper thought this gesture was a big favor.

Rodrigo didn't argue, even though he wasn't driving distracted. Rather, he was only laughing while driving. The minivan was sitting on the speed limit, straight within its lane. Jerome was talking, detailing the seitan protein loaf served in prison, with its trapped bits of re-hydrated corn and peas, and how it was used for purposes other than eating. Like ear muffs. Or busts groomed into prison Chia Pets. Laughing at seitan, that's what they were doing when the state troopers in an unmarked cruiser pulled alongside, looked in, and saw three occupants, two brown and one black, having fun that abruptly ceased when the presence of authority was noticed.

None of the three knows how much time the steaks need over the campfire. Jerome gets impatient twirling, and after five minutes decides to nibble the cooked edges then return the rare back to the flame.

"Like döner kebab," points out Aziz.

"Donna who?" asks Jerome.

"Döner kebab. It's the best street food in Germany," explains Aziz. "The meat is on a, um, how do you say it? The meat is on a post that is turning around a grill. The outside that's cooked is sliced off and eaten on pita bread."

"Peter bread," repeats Jerome.

"Sounds like tacos al pastor," offers Rodrigo.

Interstate Grill

The minivan labors pathetically over the Rockies at 45 mph, hogging the right lane. The engine finds the endless grade and thinner oxygen at this altitude not to its liking. Rodrigo could push it to 50 but the dare of damage doesn't seem worth the extra nudge. The stereo is off, everyone is quiet, keeping an ear to the 17-year-old engine, hoping the strain doesn't pop a valve and send it into an irregular rhythm. They remain like that for almost two hours.

Cresting the Continental Divide, the minivan gathers pep on the eastern down slope. The riders' worry turns to enthusiasm, and there is consensus that a celebration is in order. They decide the steaks should be cooked in a dignified manner. At the first sign of suburban Denver they exit the freeway and find a Safeway.

With supplies and beer, they drive south racing the stretching shadow of the Rockies. They pull into a rest stop just as the sun is totally sunk by the mountains, leaving the sky plated with a goodbye of gold. There are only two other cars parked and no one is using the public grills or picnic tables.

Rodrigo makes a pyramid of charcoal briquettes in the

rest stop grill and soaks it generously with lighter fluid. The leaping flame makes him feel like a warlock. The three, with cans of beer, stand around the fire admiring it, and take turns feeding it lighter fluid.

A large SUV with license plates declaring the Missouri motto pulls in next to the minivan. Four college kids, three gals and a guy, spill out in a daze that only hours of highway miles can induce. After a few minutes scratching their heads and mumbling among themselves, they approach the crew with friendly smiles.

The young man says, "Sure is a beautiful night."

"Sure is," replies Rodrigo.

The two groups exchange howdies and introductions.

"We were wondering, and it's cool if you say no," says the young man, "but we don't have any charcoal and, after you guys have finished, of course, if we could use your grill to heat our beans and corn."

"Well, come now, you don't have to wait for our old heat," says Jerome. "Join us, break bread, we got plenty of steak and fixin's. We could have a feast with those beans."

The Missouri gang appreciate the kind invite and accept, and the two crews join for the night.

Everyone contributes to the prepping. Yams and jacket potatoes, poblano peppers to char, mighty frisbee portabella mushrooms topped with garlic butter, corn cobs to steam in their own green husks, and a pot of black beans ready to bubble. Alongside a dozen fancy steaks, the grill is stuffed and in constant rotation under the charge of Rodrigo.

On the picnic table, a giant watermelon and two cantaloupes crown the center. One of the Missouri crew, a hippie gal with dreadlocks, says she'll look around to see if there's any dandelion greens and wild carrot to zest the salad. Aziz offers his help and the two walk the perimeter of the rest area with flashlight. Sometimes they are heard giggling. A jug of wine is passed around and Jerome has good helpings of it as he stands next to Rodrigo, facetiously assisting the grilling.

When the cooking is complete, everyone is comfortable and warm with drink, seated closely around a picnic table illuminated by the glow of a camping lamp. Overloaded plates wait before each of them. Jerome quiets everyone. "We should give grace to Jesus," he says.

"But I'm Jewish," says the young man.

"Well, that's cool, because when it comes down to it, giving thanks has nothing to do with religion. Jesus. Allah. Moses. Buddha. Kanye. All the same," says Jerome.

"Indeed," affirms Aziz.

Jerome bows his head, and everyone follows. "We give thanks," says Jerome, "to this here bounty before us. Thanks to Mother Earth. Thanks for new friends. And thanks to freedom." Jerome pauses before saying amen.

They all cheer, then dig into a grand feast, leaving them with taut bellies.

After dinner, one of the college gals plays ukulele. There is drink and song, and Jerome tries to beat box but runs out of breath and laughs, and everyone laughs along. Aziz sees fireflies and gives chase with the hippie gal joining him. "Don't touch 'em, Azizy!" yells Jerome, "They lose their light when you do!"

The festivities go late and by the early morning hours only Jerome and the gal with the ukulele remain awake. Jerome is lying on the table. The ukulele gal asks, "What are you looking at?"

"I'm trying to see constellations."

"You know them?"

"Oh, yeah, sure." Jerome points. "That's the Big Dipper."

The gal twists her head awkwardly. It's uncomfortable, so she stretches herself beside Jerome. "Where?" she asks.

"Straight up."

She follows his finger and sees it. "And Orion's Belt?"

Jerome points to a set of stars lined in a row. "Right next to the Minotaur."

"Really? You mean Taurus?"

"Sure. There the horns," he says, connecting dots with his finger and making an outline. "And that's the nose ring."

"What?"

Jerome continues to gesture. "And there's the Hockey Stick. Just below the Hips of Beyoncé."

She elbows him in the ribs. They both laugh. Looking a little harder she exclaims, "Ha! I can see it! I can see the Hips of Beyoncé!" She scans the heavens and points out other constellations, such as the High Five Hand Cluster, the Scooby Doo, and Jackson Pollock. Jerome doesn't know who Jackson Pollock is but, with the warmth of a woman next to him, he laughs just the same.

NIAGARA
AKIMBO

I admit there was a time when I spray-painted myself silver, stood limp on an upturned washtub, and remained motionless until a tourist dropped money into the tip jar. This activated my robot dance. I wore reflective sunglasses because I had no idea what to do with my eyes. Heh. *Amateur.* I did that for years. Embarrassing. It's good to recognize past folly, though. It gives a chance to admire progress.

What made my folly more folly-full is that I mimed the dopey robot dance at Niagara Falls, from a vista point on the Canadian side, where the hotels, casino, wax museum, and souvenir shops glean tourists. Like them, I didn't question if roboting was appropriate or related to the awe of Niagara. I just saw a great spot to turn some cash. See, I told you, back then I had no idea what to do with my eyes.

It was a couple of years ago when all that ceased. I was preparing to start for the day, about to smear my face silver, when I noticed something walking upriver, along the Canadian shore. Even from a distance I could tell that its head was too large. It then turned to the river and walked on it, as if walking on water was natural.

As it strolled towards Horseshoe Falls, I got a better view. It had the head of an elephant and body of a man. Shirtless. Muscular, but in an old-guy type of way, like Jack LaLanne or Joseph Pilates. Blinking hard and rubbing my eyes didn't change what I was seeing. Definitely an old-timey strongman's body and definitely elephant faced. Its trunk swung at its knees, ears fanned like radar.

I attempted to draw attention to the creature, calling on tourists to witness. They turned to where I was pointing then looked back puzzled. I got more emphatic in pointing, extending both arms, shaking. "The elephant!" I yelled. "Walking across the waterfall!"

The creature was lolly-gagging along the edge of Horseshoe Falls, sucking up water in its trunk and shooting a fountain above its head. Then it noticed my waving. It waved back.

"It's waving at me! That, that... elephant thing!" But no one else could see it. The creature thought my efforts ridiculous, laughed, then broke out into a hula dance. But it had trouble doing it because it was too busy laughing at my attempts to get others to see the spectacle. When it dawned on me that no one else could see it, I gave up my efforts.

This annoyed the creature. It turned red, began to grow, to 20 feet high, transforming into a thick serpent, with a mouth as wide as its throat and ringed with a procession of pointy teeth. From the serpent's body, popping pustules birthed little mini-versions of itself that remained latched via umbilical cords. The creature and its cronies flew high, then dove at great speed, wailing like a World War Two

Nazi dive bomber, aiming itself directly at the capacity-filled Maiden of the Mist #7 ferry, chugging bravely in the lagoon at the bottom of the Falls. I restarted calling alarm, trying to draw attention to the horror charging from above. At the height of my frantic urgency, a force wrapped my body, preventing any movement.

I was rendered frozen.

At the last second, mere yards from decimating the ferry, the creature pulled-up and levitated towards me. It shape-shifted itself back into the elephant-head, man-body, and sniffed me with its trunk.

Still, tourists didn't see it. But they noticed me, frozen in an extreme frantic state, a split-second before doom. My neck veins were growling, tendons strained. Eyes about to burst, too, stunned to look away and flee. Chest at high heave. One arm almost bursting out of its socket from waving alarm. The other arm beginning to recede to defend my face from impending Maiden of the Mist shrapnel.

Vacationers emptied their pockets, opened wallets, took snapshots, framed themselves alongside for selfies. I put all effort into movement but failed. While this was happening, the creature was sitting on the ledge reading a newspaper, just in line of my periphery.

After a couple of hours of complete stillness, the creature stood, walked over, lit a cigarillo, and puffed smoke in my face. "You are quite good if you focus," she said in a chesty voice. "My name is Gladiola. I can help. Next time, be ready." Then she sprinted up-river, her strides reducing the rapids to the likes of a running machine set on geriatric.

With Gladiola gone, the spell broke, I lost balance and fell, with sweat and labored breath. The circling tourists were not expecting movement but after the gasps came laughter. I stuffed all my gear into my backpack and ran to the border. Arriving at the US checkpoint perspiring a torrent with the left side of my face twitching uncontrollably could have been a problem, but Bill was on duty. He knew I was a regular. "Brother, you look like you are coming down with a cold or something," he said. After a quick scan of my passport, he waived me through and suggested I go home and get some chicken soup.

I usually take the bus back home from the Falls but that day I walked the three miles. I had to remain moving, sitting on a bus impossible. Motion was wound inside, demanding to unwind. At home, I packed the water pipe and ripped through several bowls of cannabis before getting comfortable enough to sit and relax on the sofa. I turned on the TV, got lost in some crappy show while counting the day's haul. It was a record. Quadrupled my previous best for less than a half-day's work.

I didn't return to the Falls for a week. Too scared. But as time distanced itself from the encounter, the fear wore off. I considered all the ramifications. Was I going mad? Perhaps I should see a doctor. But then I noticed the pile of cash on the coffee table. I reached a new level of performance that I never imagined possible. The money was a testament to a budding skill-set.

So, I returned with my washtub and set up early, at dawn, without the silver paint. Separating the furious, cascading Horseshoe Falls like drapery, Gladiola appeared, yawning, stretching, and blinking her eyes. Then she saw me and levitated to the vista where I was standing. "What took you so long?" she asked, while jabbing me in the chest with her multi-ringed index finger.

I gulped. "I'm... I'm here... Now."

She wrapped her trunk around my waist, exposing her genitals. She blinked rapidly, gave bedroom eyes, angling her elephant head coyly. In overwhelmed naiveté and fear, I cringed. That's when Gladiola chose to freeze me.

It was so early that no one was around, and the giant choir of the Falls was pure, unadulterated by dissonant tourists. I was facing the deep collapse of water, stuck in a reaction of repulse. About 15 minutes later, a park attendant sweeping bits of trash into a dustpan, approached bemused, and said, "It's a little early to start, don't you think?" He swept around me, then moved on.

Tourists trickled in, the first dozen a little taken back until they realized I was a street performer. To them, it looked like the Falls were causing an earthquake and I was bracing for a severe tremor. Eyes wincing as if between a vice. Teeth clamped and grimaced. Palms raised, fingers extended like exclamations. Shoulders reaching for ears. The spike of neck hair.

I was a hit with the tourists. At the end of the third hour, Gladiola reappeared, sniffed, and looked at my tip jar. She kicked it a little. "The cup over-filleth, eh? Good for you!" and she slapped my ass with her trunk, causing me to jump in the air, startling the gathered tourists. An applause and a smattering of bravo replaced the surprise. More money.

I collected the cash, bowed, repeatedly, over-emphatic. It was like I didn't know how to stop bowing. Gladiola placed her trunk on my shoulder. "Settle," she said. "You need to walk it off," and she led us on a path upriver. From a fanny pack she offered a sports drink. "Here, you should start drinking these. Electrolytes and shit."

I downed the bottle in one swig. "How did you do that, you know, freeze me?" I spluttered. "And... and... where did you come from? Are you real?"

"So many dumb questions. Who, where, how, why, yadda yadda yadda," responded Gladiola. "Here, you need another one," and from her trunk she unloaded another sports drink. "Come on, you're walking so fast we might as well jog."

My body over-rode cognitive thinking, insisting to run alongside Gladiola instead of letting my brain fully process. I would quickly discover that maintaining movement post performance was the required balance.

"The only question is The What," said Gladiola.

"What?"

Gladiola looked at me with a raised eyebrow. Her eyelashes were long. "Are you fucking with me?"

"What do you mean?" I asked.

She stopped running. I paused with her but remained jogging in place. I was waiting for a response to my answer when Gladiola slapped my face. Not hard, but with ninja quickness. "That is the sound of one hand slapping," she said. "What does it feel like?"

I was more surprised than feeling its sting. "I don't know. I can't really think at the moment. I have to keep running."

Gladiola shook her head in disgust. "Sheesh. You have no appreciation of WHAT is happening right now. Like everybody else. Rushing hither and dither, picking up groceries, emailing spreadsheets, glowing in smart screens."

I kept quiet. I was satisfied with jogging. It felt good.

"Next time you are frozen in position, maybe– instead of fighting it–maybe you should focus on what is happening."

"Nothing," I replied. "I was frozen. I was doing nothing."

"Heh. *Amateur.* Ignorance is no way to live. Just try to think about all this tomorrow, while you're *en pose,* as the French say."

The next day, before zapping me to stillness, Gladiola instructed to stand on the washtub in triumph, like a super hero who saved the world. Or a returning general. Or an explorer declaring discovery. I set arms akimbo. Head turned, offering a rigid profile. Eyes that cut deep, peering into, and assured of, the future.

In this state of statue, I remembered what Gladiola previously said and contemplated what I was doing. *I am frozen looking like champ.* Then I wondered what I'd eat for dinner. Maybe slum it, order pizza, watch TV. *Ooh, a good night for TV, too. Or set the DVR and call Kate. Haven't seen her in a while. Maybe grab a drink with her. I wonder if she got a new job. I'll certainly have cash to splash.*

Then I'd try to move to see if the fix was still in. It was.

How come I don't get an itch? What if I do get an itch? I decided not to think about an itch because I didn't want to encourage one. Then I wondered whatever happened to Josh Middleton, my best friend in middle-school, who moved to Atlanta. I was interrupted reminiscing when a group of college kids came by, some of the gals I found cute, and they posed alongside, mimicking my stance. I tried to move my eyes to get a better view of the gals, but I had to settle with the edge of my vision.

I went on thinking like this until Gladiola dropped from the sky, landed in front of me, and touched my nose with the tip of her trunk. Instantly, over-loaded with potential energy, I jumped high and fist pumped the sky, like a beaming anime character coming to life. The gathered tourists oohed, ahhed, and clapped. I acknowledged them with a wave and a continuous, uncontrollable nod of my head. Bobble-like. After securing my belongings, Gladiola and I started our brisk walk.

"How long was I frozen?" I asked.

"About 45 minutes." She yawned.

"Is that all? Let's go back. I can do more."

She shook her head. "No, you can't."

"Sure, I can. I can make more money."

"You are such a tool."

"Huh?"

Gladiola stopped walking and pulled me in with her trunk. She bent down so her forehead touched mine. "What were you supposed to do today?" she asked.

"Hey! I didn't fight it."

"You did some but that wasn't the point."

"I just wanted to see if I was still frozen."

"Yeah?" She coiled her trunk tighter around my waist. "What were you doing while you were frozen, then?"

"I wasn't fighting it."

"You were thinking about dinner. Or what's on TV. Going out for drinks. Bills. Then those college gals came along and you tried to spy cleavage. That's what you were doing." Gladiola then whipped her trunk with a grunt of disgust.

I didn't comprehend. "Well, yeah. So what?"

"That's what you are thinking about? A mythical, glorious creature appears and entrusts you with the power of motionless and you think about breasts and pizza?" She was really steaming. "Philistine! Moronic!" she roared. "In simpleton terms, lame bullshit!" I didn't realize until then just how much she was annoyed. She turned hotter shades of red, then fizzed into vapor, steamed skyward, gone in the air.

Gladiola was there the following day, though. And in a better mood. Before I commenced, she instructed that I do some stretches. "You should also do yoga," she said.

I contorted and struck a yoga position.

"What the fuck is that?" asked Gladiola.

"Fighting Crane, from the movie *Karate Kid*." I was standing on one leg, my arms raised over my head, arched like grand antlers. Gladiola froze me.

I metaphysically kicked myself, my *Karate Kid* prank an open invitation for Gladiola. I needed to be mindful of my actions. She was keen on identifying moments of weakness. I was tempted to try defreezing, a little concerned at how long I could stand on one leg but figured that if I got tired, I'd just tip over. It wasn't as if my leg would fall off. Then my mind began to wander but I eventually caught it red-handed and cut the meander, trying to appreciate Gladiola's advice.

What am I doing right now? Breathing. That wasn't frozen. And my pulse. A vein undulating to the rhythm of my heart. A pair of pores slowly plonking forth a bead of oily sweat on my forehead. Was that my liver doing something? And there...there is the length of my intestines.

As I started to examine and realize how much was happening, Gladiola approached unknown from behind and slapped my ass with her trunk. I flew out of Fighting Crane like a starburst, higher than I have ever jumped before.

Where gravity and thrust cancel each other out, I see

tourists along the railing, pressing screens, focusing faces, framing the Falls as backdrop. Attention to touch screens is interrupted by my unexpected, spectacular jump and those nearby turn and look, their mouths round like small black holes. Past them is the Niagara river, a raging rush of water that not only has the rug pulled out from under its feet but also the floor, basement, and 300 feet of bedrock. The river leaps valiantly but is widely surprised, succumbs to gravity, and plummets like an infinite column into a mist of its own debris.

THE EXIT

A large Australian mining magnate sits across the table from me. He's round like a proud cheeseburger. The armpits of his beige polo shirt accounts his progression of sweat. He raises $490,000 and lounges deep into the upholstery of his chair, the same easy way the fat of his jowls swell and overwhelm his neck. Confident, that's the way I read him. He's likely got the high pair. Backed by a second pair, too. The magnate is attempting to maintain a blank face, but I see what he looked like half a century ago, when he was a doughy, rosy cheeked child about to dig into a big bowl of pudding.

Magnate is expecting a win but I'm delivering his loss. I pulled a gut shot straight.

Still, there's something wrong.

Magnate coughs, unhinges phlegm, and launches it into the spittoon. Seventeen hours ago, after introductions and settling himself into his chair, the first thing the magnate complains about is the lack of a spittoon. Nevada is the wild west, he asserts, and a spittoon is not only appropriate

41

but expected, especially in the high-roller room. The casino management profusely agreed and within minutes a brass spittoon was given its own seat next to the magnate. It is drained and cleaned every hour.

Taking money from the likes of him usually feels good. But I am really bothered by the magnate's unpleasantness. He mostly eats deviled eggs. He's nibbled on other things like pâté, caviar, hot wings, and popcorn, but he always rounds off with a deviled egg. It is hard to ignore his yolk colored teeth. I tried striking a conversation around midnight, searching for redeeming qualities, such as wife and children. But he ended up bragging about his womanizing, concluding, "Me and the missus have an arrangement. I don't tell her about it, and she doesn't know." He thought this was hilarious and boomed a laugh, launching a masticated bit of egg onto my face.

I expect the moment of victory – the glory of the jackpot, it's wealth, the establishment of who's really top dog – to dissolve all the unpleasantness I've had to put up with. It usually does. But this time, I am finding little satisfaction.

There are no windows in the high roller room. The air doesn't have a chance to smell or venture away from 72.5 degrees and 32% humidity. The lighting is subdued, ambers and browns warm the decor. It's supposed to carry the refinement of a Victorian era Gentleman's Club but there's too much veneer and effort, and it comes across as dry cleanable.

The staff are Professional. Personalities starched into service. No more than *yes sir* and *would you care for something else, sir.* They are not there for conversation.

Just outside the room, a suited employee stands over a

podium, guarding the roped-off entrance. He's connected, wearing a Bluetooth ear piece. Beyond the rope, battalions of slot machines in maze formation, stainless steel and glowing plastics with chimes and bells, bullies of disorientation suckering true believers into giving up their retirement. The slots must be negotiated before finding the casino's discrete exit.

Outside the building, the air is scorched, the wide sidewalks double-down the sun, the high-rise battalion of resort hotels reflect more. Wandering masses, families strolling from one theme to the next, snapping selfies before faux New York skyline, faux Eiffel Tower, and the water fountain show of Bellagio.

As I call the magnate's raise, I consider all the places where I have bet, and confirm this high-roller room goes down as the least pleasurable, the flattest of all. Even with the large pot, I should be somewhere else. Anywhere is better. I remember a bingo hall in Texarkana, the Arkansas side, operating out of a highway strip-mall, where the numbered balls are plucked by the white gloved hand of an old southern belle then held high for everyone to see, while her retiree husband wearing a bolo tie announces the number and incorporates a rhyme: "Twenty-two, twenty-two, tonight I ate pork chili stew," or, "forty-eight, forty-eight, tomorrow is Sunday, don't show to church late." And the big jackpot everyone is excited about; the platter of meat provided by H.E.B that has five pounds of sausage, a stack of pork chops, and two sides of fatty brisket.

Seeing my cards and confirmation from the dealer of my superior hand, the Australian mining magnate is a boiling beetroot. He is raging protest, bits of egg spit fly. Abruptly, before reaching the peak of his fury, he is cut silent, his face strained with contortion, and he falls flat to the floor, grasping his left shoulder.

There's a portable defibrillator in the high-roller room, the staff trained to operate it. The magnate's polo shirt is cut with a pair of scissors and sensors are stickered onto his egg white chest. The machine whirls into charge and before someone commands *Clear!* I have left the room, begun the trek to the casino exit, whispering a rhyme under my breath.

THE BRIM OF LOS ANGELES

Camarón que se duerme se lo lleva la corriente – A dicho, a proverbial saying from Mexico, that translates to shrimp that falls asleep is swept away by the current.

Entering the freeway, the windshield wipers were at full swing. It was obvious the rain clouds were set to lounge the entire day over the Los Angeles basin. Ben Sardine shot a glance to the rear-view mirror. It was tilted to the back seat, where layers of blankets covered a lifeless mound. "Maybe we should wait and bury him tomorrow," suggested Sardine. "We can get some ice."

In the passenger seat, with a half-bottle of tequila on his lap, Pryor waved away the concern, mumbling, "I know my shit, keep driving," and took a long swig. Sardine didn't argue. If grave digging in a downpour was what his friend wanted then he would be there to help. The driving was slow, the rain tempering speed, and it took an hour before they reached the San Gabriel mountains. It was here where the Los Angeles sprawl petered-out; the subdivision designed homes and strip-malls unable to overcome the steep terrain. Proving Pryor did indeed know the peculiarities of local weather patterns, once they reached the crest of the mountain pass the sky cleared, revealing an unhindered, shameless sun presiding over a high-desert plateau. Everything looked aged with a pale brown hue running through it all – the dirt, the desert scrub, the horizon all dipped in weak sepia. Sparse stands of Joshua trees populated either side of the highway. Their battered reach to the heavens culminated with an exhausted attempt at greenery, appearing like desert geriatrics wearing moth-eaten wigs. Tough clumps of wiry grass and shrubs lived in their shadows, eking out a meek living. The water on the car quickly evaporated and a thin coat of desert dust replaced it. There were no other cars on the road – they were the only things moving. On a map, 50 miles away as the crow flies, the commotion of downtown Los Angeles was in full flex.

This part of the world wasn't always so still. Great herds of antelope once roamed. There was enough vegetation for them to live on, spread over a vast area. On seeing these herds, the European settlers chose the obvious and named the region Antelope Valley. An ice-storm in the late Spring of 1844 caught the nursing antelopes by surprise and killed more than half their numbers. Settlers harvested as much meat from the carcasses as they could, filling their cellars with jerky and salted cuts, but supply overwhelmed and, the following week, the entire valley held the funk of rot. More settlers arrived in the succeeding decades, bringing cattle, irrigation and farms which looked like gluttonous oases to the antelope. This drew the ire of the farmers and the animals were hunted to near oblivion. The great herds have long gone and, today, an actual antelope in Antelope Valley is a rare sight.

The car was cruising at 65 when they both saw the buck a quarter-mile ahead, standing at attention beside the highway. Sardine pointed to it and was about to express how strange it was to see such a majestic creature in such a nothing place, but Pryor spoke over him. "You need to slow down, man." Sardine had time enough to respond with a "huh?" when the buck's sense of alarm went haywire and bolted towards the car instead of fleeing. Sardine slammed the brakes, swerving onto the gravel shoulder. The car spun in circles before managing to gain grip and stop. The buck continued running down the highway for a few hundred yards then dashed into the desert scrub.

"Chingao, vato!" yelled Pryor. The bottle of tequila had spilled onto his groin and fallen to floor, where it trickled out to empty. Sardine continued to grip the steering wheel, white-knuckled, his glasses unhooked from one ear and resting diagonally across his blood-drawn face. Everything that wasn't belted down was thrown askew. The mound on the back seat was free from the blankets and now lay on the arm-rest between Sardine and Pryor. An overweight dog, a multi-breed mutt, with its tongue hanging out like a deflated balloon.

*****

Be-speckled and blue-eyed was Ben Sardine, with a half-grown goatee and a haircut too short that made his head seem wide. Could pass for handsome if he gave his mop half a chance. A year ago, just after graduating from high-school with average grades and absolutely zero desire for college, Sardine packed bags into his Hyundai and left suburban Dallas, hitting the road westward.

It was well into the sprawl of Riverside County but miles away from Los Angeles proper, stuck in a freeway traffic jam, that the car overheated and began steaming like a train. Sardine managed to conjure the car to an exit ramp where it cut-out, but carried enough momentum to roll into a busy gas station that also served as a diner and gift shop. It was late Sunday afternoon, finding a mechanic impossible, so Sardine got a room at the chain motel next door and ate at the diner.

The next day, the car was towed to a mechanic, where an unexpected price was quoted, dealing a serious dent to his savings. Later, returning to the diner, contemplating calling his family to send him money, he noticed the **HELP WANTED** sign on the front door. That night, he started his first shift as a graveyard dishwasher.

The graveyard cook was Richard Pryor. Richard Pryor wasn't and certainly didn't look anything like the famous comedian. Pryor, the cook, was five foot six, in his late fifties, carried a significant amount of fat around his midriff, and, most notable of the differences between him and his famous namesake, was of Mexican descent. Although mostly gray, his hair was still thick and lush, and he slicked it back just as he did as a young man. No one knew his real name. Sardine thought it was his real name. He'd never heard of the comedian Richard Pryor.

No one could deny Pryor's cooking skills. It was understood by all employees, from busboys to management, that Pryor was the diner's best cook. He was fast and efficient, but always moved with cool ease, shuffling back and forth from hotplate to cutting board to oven at a Sunday stroll pace. His food tasted better than the other cooks. Even the toast. Eggs were his specialty. Pryor proclaimed that an omelet was a chance for the cook to make a chicken fly. Rumors circulated among the waitstaff that Pryor trained at a fancy New York City culinary school and worked in restaurants featured in travel and food cable channels.

Pryor was happy with the job's low expectations and uncomplicated menu. The slowness of the graveyard shift afforded lengthy smoke breaks in the back alley, where he set up a folding chair and an upturned milk crate served as a table. Here, he played his version of solitaire called *Oveja Negra*, under the emergency exit light, with a cigarette hanging from the corner of his mouth. Other times he would put his feet up, peer into the night, trying to make out stars that managed to shine through the freeway lights. It was also where the dog waited and snoozed, waking when Pryor emerged from the kitchen door, wagging its tail for the expected piece of hamburger or pork chop bone. And this was how Sardine was introduced to the dog. It was his first shift. Sardine was scraping a pork chop into the trash and Pryor noticed. "Hey man," said Pryor, "get that bone out of there and take it outside."

"Huh?" said Sardine.

"That bone you just trashed. Do me a solid, man, and take it to the alley out back."

Sardine thought it an odd request and paused.

"Listen, man... say, what's your name again?"

"Ben. Ben Sardine."

"Sardine. What? Man alive, what is that, Jewish?"

"No. Uh... I'm from Texas."

Pryor took a hard look at his new dishwasher. "Well,

hell sheeit, of course you are. Do me a favor, Tex, I'd appreciate it if you pull that bone and mosey on out to the alley."

"Sure... uh... okay..." and thinking it as some sort of initiation, Sardine retrieved the bone and did like he was told.

The dog woke up from beside the milk crate and wagged its tail, seeing the bone treasure in Sardine's hand. "Hey there, fella," Sardine said disarmingly. The dog stood up, already open-mouthed, licking his chops, eagerly panting. Sardine lobbed the bone toward the dog who caught it and began to gnaw. "Good catch!" he said and approached to pat the dog. But the hound didn't want interruption and vice-gripped down on the bone, growled and, from the corner of its eyes, cut a glare at Sardine. Sardine backed away slowly, retreating to the kitchen.

"That's Loquito," said Pryor. "I bet he likes you now."

"I don't think so," said Sardine. "He growled."

"Sheeit, man, don't worry about that, that's just instinct. He's fucking with you. That dog has never bit no one out of anger. Here, let's all go outside and we'll settle this right now."

Back out in the alley, the dog was still gnawing. "Look, watch," said Pryor, and he walked up to the dog, bent over him, and grabbed the bone. The dog growled, refusing to let go. Pryor pulled, the dog countered, all the while growling in heightened intensity. They tug o' warred for a spell, and then Pryor relented, laughing. "See. Just instinct, all motherfucker show." Unfolding his chair, he simultaneously fished-out a bottle of Old Crow from behind a drainage pipe. "I usually don't drink at work but... well, what the fuck, eh? To your first day on the job." He took a swig and turned the bottle to Sardine.

Sardine hesitated but grimaced a slug. He didn't want to appear rude.

*****

Ben Sardine stepped on the shoulder of a shovel, pushing its blade into the earth, beside a Joshua tree that reached higher than its neighbors. They were fairly sure it was the same place where, nine months ago, they spent a day in the desert frolicking while Pryor smoked bacon. He scored a slab of pork belly and a bundle of mesquite from a Cajun trucker. "You can't smoke bacon in city limits," said Pryor. "The smell drives everyone nuts. Old Wynona would bitch and moan all day," he said, referring to the landlady. "We need to start early and go smoke it in the desert. We don't want to be smokin' bacon when it gets dark. That's when the coyotes get brave."

The first few shovel stabs into the desert were easy, the top six inches loose, mostly crumbling dried detritus of plants working their way back into elemental minerals. But it gave way to a hard, compact layer. Sardine made a few scratches at it, then stopped. "That's some tough desert rock," he said. He heaved the shovel with force into the excavation, the shovel rang, his tight grip released. Sardine shook his hands in the air to relieve the jarring sting, letting the tool fall to the ground.

Pryor placed his six pack of beer against the tree. "What the fuck you doing?" he asked, and moved to the hole to take over the dig. His leg was like a ratchet, stepping with force and mechanical efficiency, plunging the shovel deep, freeing large clumps. "Shieeet. This ain't bad," he said, and continued digging while talking. "In Alaska, they got permafrost. You know what that shit is?" Sardine shrugged his shoulders as he freed a beer from the six-pack. "It's frozen earth. Rock solid and that motherfucker don't crack open for no thing less than a hundred pound jackhammer."

"What do you mean frozen?" asked Sardine.

"Frozen is frozen. Gets so cold up there everything freezes. You can throw boiling water in the air and before it hits the ground it turns into snow. The ground freezes, too. That's permafrost."

"So how do they bury people? Use a jackhammer?"

"They wait till summer. Some tribes have been known to bury the dead in trees. Mostly cremation, though. Heat is precious and welcomed." Pryor speared the shovel in the hole, leaving the handle upright and waiting. "I'm too old for this shit. I drink beer, you dig. When I was your age I could swing a shovel all day then fuck steady all night."

The sun's reach was stretching higher and broader, but the desert wasn't as still – a breeze picked-up every few moments, carrying an inkling of welcoming coolness, dulling the brash sun, giving the spinifex and the Joshua tree fronds a rare shake. Sardine resumed digging duties, concentrating on his form, imitating Pryor, letting his legs do the work, and finally started making progress.

"I always wanted to cook a pig in the ground, buried in embers," said Pryor, wiping the sweat from his brow with his beer can. "A suckling. I wanted to do it when we were here last time but that's a lot of meat for the three of us. And then you have to get a lot of river rocks to mix into the embers to retain heat, like they do in Hawaii."

"The bacon was plenty," said Sardine between swings,

"It lasted a month."

"I forgot to bring the pool." Pryor was referring to the small inflatable kiddie pool that he brought the previous visit. While the bacon was in the smoker, Pryor was in his underwear, lounging in the pool, puffing joints of Mexican brick weed. Pryor quietly "borrowed" three 12-gallon tanks from the diner's water cooler back-stock to supply the pool. Loquito enjoyed the pool, too, being able to soak and lap at the same time. The highlight of the day for the dog, though, was chasing a young hare and catching it. Everyone was impressed. Perhaps the dog was surprised the most. Once having captured his prey, he was at a loss, and resorted to yelping at the stunned animal. Pryor insisted enough was enough, put the dog on a leash, and returned him to the pool, rewarding him with a bowl of beer. Loquito settled, spent the rest of the day sprawled in the pool, enjoying stray drafts of Mexican brick weed, resting his head on Pryor's knee, soaking, lapping, snoring.

Pryor was looking towards the mountain crest to the south, the sky behind it thickening with darker clouds. But his eyes were looking at the memory of the inflatable pool, the hare, the happy dog, all in the air of bacon smoke. "That was a beautiful day," Pryor said. It looked like he was about to cry but his eyes returned to focus. He gulped down the half-can remaining, and turned to Sardine. "We have to hurry. Let me loosen it up a little and you shovel it out."

*****

By his fifth dishwasher shift at the diner, Sardine was greeted by the dog with a wag so emphatic that its hind quarters wobbled in the tail's wake. The dog appreciated Sardine slipping him prime morsels. No bare bones, always bones with meat. That night, a barely eaten T-bone made its way to the dirty plate stacks. Sardine was tempted to finish it, and was pondering why it was wrong to eat another person's discarded food. Pryor noticed Sardine's widening eyes on the steak and promised the new dishwasher a steak of his own – there was no way anyone in his kitchen would eat scraps. So Sardine took the near complete t-bone to the alley, away from temptation, and to a dog that lit up with a wobbly rear and attentive ears. Sardine and Loquito playfully wrestled for it. Pryor followed outside for a smoke and noticed the play.

"Man, that dog has taken a shine to you."

Sardine relinquished the t-bone steak and the mutt took the bone next to the milk crate, settled down, and began chewing and gnawing. "You know, I didn't think much of Loquito before," said Sardine. "He kind of scared me at first. But that's misconceptions for you. He's sweet."

"Important for a man to befriend at least one domesticated beast," said Pryor. "I'm not saying you should go out and get a dog now. You're too young, you got other things to do, maintain responsibilities to yourself."

"I can't have a dog where I'm living anyways."

"Where do you live?"

"Next door."

"What do you mean you live next door?" asked Pryor. He searched his memory, discarded the strip-mall. "You're not talking about the Super 8?"

"Yeah. Third floor. Facing the mountains," he said optimistically.

"Man, that's motherfucking dumb, with a capital D,

and might as well add a capital B, that's how motherfucking DumB it is."

"It's not bad. Water pressure is good."

"How much does that shit cost?"

"It's a hundred a night," said Sardine, without any sense of pride or shame.

"What the fuck, man? You're not going to stay there?"

"I haven't thought about it, really, but yeah, I should look for a place, I guess."

Pryor shook his head. "Look-see, I live in an apartment. It used to be a garage but its been converted. Provides money flow for the old gal who lives in the main house. There's a small loft, overlooks the living room. Give me that hunny a week and it's yours."

"Uh... well..."

"What the fuck are you contemplating with *uh* and *well*. It's a good deal for both of us. I get money. You save money."

"I need to take a look first."

"Sure, come by tomorrow. But seriously, you'll see, it's great."

Sardine then froze with a realization. "I've already paid for three more nights at the motel."

"What the fuck, man? Cancel it. Get your green back."

"I don't know if I can."

"What? It's your money, you haven't used their services."

"I guess."

"You guess? Don't be so foolish with cash."

The next day, in the afternoon, Sardine walked to Pryor's. It was a mile a way, in a suburb filled with 1950's homes that sat on quarter acre lots, with long front yards and wide paved driveways. Pryor's address was a small two-story house with light blue aluminum siding, dents showing here and there. As Sardine followed the driveway back to the garage apartment, a side door to the house swung open and an old lady appeared, brandishing in her pale and liver-spotted hands a broom. "Who are you?" she spat in a southern accent. "I tell you before that I recycle my own cans and bottles. It's m' money. Now you go on... get!" She might have reached four foot ten, thin like a wintering fruit tree, her mouth only holding bottom dentures. Her long gray hair was bundled in a bun constructed a couple of days before. She was wearing a pink tracksuit that looked fresh from the dryer.

Sardine stopped and raised his hands as if to ease a wild horse. "Sorry to interrupt, ma'am," he said. "I'm here to see Richard."

She took a good look at him. So clean shaved he probably has never shaved, she thought.

"Pryor. Richard Pryor," said Sardine louder. "Your tenant... lives out back."

"I've never seen you before."

"I work with Richard. At the diner. My name is Ben Sardine."

"What?"

"I work at the diner with Richard."

"You said something about red sardines. Don't deny it. I heard yous. I don't know what it means and I'm not keen on learnin'."

"No... sorry, ma'am," and pausing to raise his voice, "I said my name is Benjamin Sardine."

The old lady looked at him hard, wrinkled her nose, sniffed the air.

"I'm from Dallas."

"That's where they killed the President. Hasn't been the same since."

"No ma'am, it hasn't."

Richard Pryor came out of the garage apartment and sized the situation immediately. "Jaysus! Wynona, put down the broom!" Pryor walked to Sardine and placed a hand on his shoulder. "This is the nephew I was talking about. He's going to stay with me for a little whiles."

Wynona lowered the broom but gave both of them a mean look. "He said he was a coworker of yours."

"Sure. I got him a job,too. He's from Texas. My sister's boy."

"You two don't look related."

"Sister from a different mother."

"Well, I hope you don't fry fish in there. It'll stink up the place. Never get the smell out." Wynona then started to sweep around the threshold.

"What you talking about, ol' gal?" asked Pryor.

"He's the one talking about fish," she said, pointing at Sardine.

"Why you talking about fish?" Pryor asked Sardine.

"I wasn't. It's just my name. I don't think..."

"Whatever, man." Pryor turned Sardine to the back. "Okay, Wynona. No fish, I know. I made meatloaf last night. You want some?" At the sound of meatloaf, the dog came out of the apartment, saw Sardine, approached and licked his hand. Loquito wasn't the only one who perked up.

"Ooh, yeah. You got mashed potatoes?" asked Wynona.

"Sure do."

"Well, don't be shy about it, I was wondering what I was going to fix for supper."

"Okay, I'll fix you a plate and bring it up at six."

"Make it six-thirty," said Wynona. "I like to eat watching Wheel."

Everyone nodded inn agreement, Pryor gestured to Sardine to walk down the driveway towards the apartment. She watched them as they entered and continued surveillance for another minute to make sure there wasn't any presence of fish.

It used to be a two-car garage with a widow peak attic but all remnants of that had disappeared, aside from the old workbench stretched along a wall, now sanded fine, oiled, and polished. The roller doors were replaced with a French door that welcomed light. Inside, a large floor plan with the kitchen, living and dining room all open to each other. It was tidy and ordered with various mementos and artwork decorating nooks and walls.

"Well, here it is. See those stairs? They go up there," said Pryor, pointing to the loft above. "It's not totally private but to be seen from down here you have to be standing right up against the railing. The back of it is dark, not much daylight. Important for us graveyard folks to maintain serotonin levels."

An old leather couch with a Pendleton blanket neatly folded over its back faced the French door. It was well worn but there were no tears nor cracking, the leather maintained and now, after carrying countless asses and drunk pass-outs, was smooth and soft.

"Man, I'm impressed," said Sardine.

"What do you mean?"

"I didn't think that..." and Sardine caught himself

before accidentally saying a disparaging remark.

"I see what your opinion of me is," said Pryor.

"Oh no! I mean... I don't know, I didn't really know what to expect. This is really cool. You got a really cool place, with cool shit, it's really..."

"Man, it's easy to break your balls," and Pryor laughed. He then walked to the kitchen and got two onions from a cupboard and threw one to Sardine. "Catch."

Sardine flinched, the onion hitting him then falling to the floor and rolling under the leather couch. "What was that!" shrieked Sardine.

"Sad motherfucker," muttered Pryor to himself. Then, "Man, it's just a motherfucking onion. I need you to dice it. We have to cook a meatloaf."

Sardine took a moment, regathered his sensibilities. "I wasn't expecting an onion to be hurled at me." He eyes trained to the floor, looking for the bulb. "I thought you cooked the meatloaf last night?"

"I was just defusing a situation. I know what that old gal likes. Besides, she could ask a lot more in rent. And she's letting you stay, and I say meatloaf is the least we could do. She thinks she's watching over me but truth is I watch over her, too. Look, I'll make it and you deliver. She'll appreciate that."

"You sure?"

"Yeah. Just reintroduce yourself and be polite this time. And, motherfucker, don't mention fish."

*****

Sardine was on his knees, working at the grave with the shovel. "Is this deep enough?" he asked.

"Another foot or so. The coyotes, motherfucking persistent, once their taste buds get a scent it likes, they go to great lengths." Pryor tapped Sardine on the shoulder and handed him a joint. "Watch it," he said. Sardine relinquished digging duties and crawled aside. Pryor stepped into the hole, plunged the shovel, and removed a large clump of dirt, depositing it outside the hole on the back swing with a twist. He continued plunging, swinging, and dumping, a routine like a pendulum – an efficient way of delivering maximum power with the least effort.

Sardine toked, propped himself on a tree, noticed it wasn't as quiet as before. The stir of the breeze more consistent, carrying on it the breath of the sea, and a distant rumble of thunder. He looked at the old man in the ditch. "Where did you learn to work a shovel? I mean, you're a machine."

"Shieet...I was born doing this. My parents, they came across the border. We grew your food." Pryor powered a dozen more shovels full then stopped. Sweat stains grew from his arm pits and seeped from rolls of fat under his chest. "It's all loose down there, you can get the rest. Here, help me out."

Sardine pulled Pryor from the hole, swapping position. Pryor finished the joint. "That's right, we grew your food," said Pryor. "Lettuce. Beans. Broccoli. Things just don't materialize and drop onto your plate. Cultivation is a constant process, constantly tending. Fucked-up, heavy work, man. I'm glad I didn't maintain the family trade. I'd probably be dead by now if I did." Looking down at Sardine in the hole, it reminded Pryor of childhood. "You see how you are on your knees like that? That's how you harvest potatoes. The combine tractor never gets all the potatoes, so we followed that farting dirt machine, on our hands and knees feeling through the churned earth, searching for missed potatoes. Shieet, every now and then you'd find a rotten one. You don't know they're rotten until you grab it and it turns to instant mush, releasing the most *ungodly* stank, man. Purifying flesh served with old hominy. And tripas. If you could smell one of those zombie TV shows, that's what it would be like. I wouldn't be surprised if the potato is the vegetable most genetically closest to humans."

"I don't think the potato is a vegetable," responded Sardine.

"Legume. Tuber. What-the-fuckever. That's not the point."

They both noticed the changing air. It was gaining more character. The rustling shimmied through the shrubbery at a heavier shake. Pieces of loose bark and failed off-shoots hanging frail from Joshua trees, fell to the ground. Tufts of dust whooped and bellowed around, scattering then reforming, an indecisive spirit debating whether to manifest or not.

Sardine got down to business, finally finding a rhythm. He cleared Pryor's digs then dug deeper until the hole rode above his knees and approached his hips. This, he knew, was deep enough. Sardine then removed all the loose dirt, squared the corners, and leveled the grave's floor.

As Sardine tidied, Pryor returned to the car, to the back seat. He removed several blankets until Loquito was unveiled. Carefully, sliding his arms underneath the dog, Pryor cradled him closely, and carried him to the grave. He knelt, and as he handed the dog to Sardine positioned in the pit, Pryor kissed the dog's forehead, whispering in its ear, "Papacito, thank you for your time." And that's when Pryor started to cry.

Sardine placed the dog with reverence, making sure Loquito's tail curled neatly, then climbed out of the grave. Pryor propped the last can of beer alongside the dog, and with Sardine's help, returned to his feet. They both stood solemnly, heads bowed. The now ever-present wind brewed even stronger, moving, shifting everything, besides the two of them, who were the only things remaining still.

Pryor broke his stance proudly. "Él era un amigo mío!" he proclaimed to the heavens. He said it again, but stronger, and stretched his arms upwards, the palms of his hands open and appealing acknowledgment.

Sardine responded. "Él era un amigo mío!"

Pryor turned to Sardine with a smile and slapped his back.

The sky over the mountains was bruised, flashes pulsated from it, a heavy roll of thunder growled. With this bold announcement, the volatile system broke over the peaks, eager to remove the desert's clear, blue sky. A large belly rain band formed, bellowing, bloating.

Sardine picked up the shovel and, while chanting "Él era un amigo mío!" began to cover the grave. Pryor smiled through his tears, joined in with the chant, pushing dirt into the grave with his foot like he was passing a soccer ball.

The mountain range was lost in fat columns of clouds. Even though it was still clear overhead, a bright flash exclaimed from the storm front and a loud charge of thunder quickly barreled over them. Pausing, the two men looked each other. "Hurry," said Pryor.

The air swirled, brooding clouds over-brooded. One

giant, thick column quickly formed above and robbed them the sun. Fat drops, minions, pelted mean, with more velocity and driven than normal rain.

"That's good enough," yelled Pryor. "Quick! Back to the car!" Pryor crouched close to the ground, squatting his way to the vehicle. Sardine ran past him, the shovel hoisted on his shoulder. Before Pryor could yell at him about conductivity and attraction, Sardine jumped into the driver's seat.

Sardine was laughing as Pryor got into the seat next to him. "Wow! This is some crazy storm," he exclaimed. The hairs on their arms stood to attention, and strands from both of their heads began to flutter upwards. Before either one could say a word, a lightning bolt struck the ground behind them, near the grave. It was a purifying, silent flash followed quickly by a ferocious crack, as if something strong and eternal, something like gravity, was snapped. They both ducked below the dash. Sardine's ears blanked, only registering a high ringing. He shook his head and felt hands shaking his shoulders. It was Pryor, who was yelling at him but he could only hear the ring.

"Chingao! You alright?! Benny! You with me! Motherfucker!"

"Huh? What?"

"You alright. Jaysus! Lets get out of here!"

"What?"

Pryor shook him again. The ringing started to subside and the sound of the world around him, the hard pelting rain, the gusts, Pryor's voice, came back, knifing through the sonic boom muffle. "Can you drive, man?"

"Yes... yes. What the fuck was that?"

"Just the motherfuckin' universe saying we should

move! Pronto!"

"Wait! Should we be in the car? Doesn't it attract lightning?"

"It's a Hyundai! Made of plastic!"

"Huh?"

"Look, the lightning will go to the engine block, probably give it some fucking power."

"What?"

"Cabrón! Ride on, man! Move!"

And Sardine slipped the car into gear, the tires spinning before gripping and speeding their getaway. Behind them, the lightning had split through the tallest Joshua tree, crystallizing its path in the sand at the head of the grave, crackling as it lost its glow.

NEW YORK CITY

When I'm rolling down the street people pause, impossible to ignore my 24 feet of American steel, the chrome grill and fenders refracting light like flash bulbs. I'm Midnight Blue, the closest blue to black, nine coats deep, like peering into an unfathomed pool. Trim crisp as the day I was born. I beam Respectability. You won't find any other hearse my age in such condition, nope, matter of fact not any other *vehicle*. That's not an easy thing to accomplish in The City. I've suffered neither ding nor scratch, not a cough of rust, bubs, I'm a fine, *fine* long-bodied stretch of machine from 1979.

That's the thing, though. I feel *too* young. I shouldn't. I should have dings and scratches. A dimple in my fender or a scrape underside, now that's character. I wish I had more miles than the 17,763. And those miles are mostly retreads from mortuary to funeral home to cemetery. I've never really been out of The City too much. Connecticut. Jersey. Up-state once.

I understand, I'm a hearse, this is what I'm supposed

69

to do. I live long and die young. But with Elijah and Eliza
retiring and closing the funeral home, I've had time to
wonder what's out there, way out west, beyond the New
Jersey turnpike.

The life of a hearse is mostly waiting on the dead. Of
all the things to wait for. The dead have no rush to be
anywhere. I don't mean to sound so jaded. I used to think,
sure, the last ride on Earth should be the sweetest and
smoothest ride that body's ever had. But after thousands
of rides, it seems a bit wasteful. The dead don't appreciate
it. The heavy-duty shocks fill the potholes and smooth the
bumps. The emerald shag in the back, and its underlay, inches
deep, soft and forgiving like a bosom. Wood paneling, even
on the ceiling, carrying the charm of an old library, with
glowing accent lights bringing out the handsome grain of
the oak. The push-button window blinds made of cherry-
wood. I carry the bouquets of countless wreaths and
floral arrangements. Decades of fresh flowers. I mention
these things because I think they are very impressive and
luxurious, deserving a nod of acknowledgement. But the
dead never appreciate anything. Unmoved. Death must be
extremely impressive.

The last couple of years, as Elijah and Eliza closed in
on their seventies, the business slowly wound down until
services were reduced to once a week. The funeral home
is equipped with three different viewing rooms, and back
in the heyday all three were used. Although there's always
business in death, none of Elijah and Eliza's children held
interest carrying on the tradition. They forged their own
careers. All college graduates. No student loans. The funeral
home has served the family well. It's in Williamsburg, and
the fashionable money is ready to pounce on any available

building. People have come and gone, inspecting. Multi-millionaire twins came in and thought the place perfect for their high-brow cocktail bar with bowling lanes. The time and money's right for Elijah and Eliza to move to a bigger house outside The City, closer to their children and grand-children.

I haven't carted the dead in three months. The last was old Maurice Basi, an icon of the neighborhood, who back in the 60s turned his parents' Italian restaurant into one of the finest pizzerias in Brooklyn. Elijah says they make the best pizza pie he's ever had, and Saturday dinner has been Basi's pizza night for as long as I've been around. The Basi's named the green olive, chicken, and extra cheese pizza, *The Elijah*. They always tip their heads and cross themselves when I roll by the pizzeria and don't care what color hands dress their dearly departed.

Maurice Basi wasn't my last trip, though. The last was something out of the ordinary. I'd been in the garage close to a month since the Basi funeral, not turned-over once in that time, the longest stretch of stillness I've endured. It was just before Memorial Day weekend. Elijah opened the garage doors, walked in whistling, ran a finger over the hood, then shook his head at the dust. A sun-beam found me, the warmth felt good, and my chrome creaked with expansion. It was only a month since I saw Elijah, but he looked a lot healthier. Younger, too. At Maurice's funeral, his age showed. Hunched, hollow cheeks, and Elijah even cried, something I've rarely seen, his eyes drooped like over-ripe fruit. But after a month into retirement, Elijah stood tall, fit, dressed neatly in polo shirt and shorts, his step as bright as his new deck shoes. His head didn't look as bald.

Elijah was impressed that I started without fuss and purred. As if I knew anything else. I was rolled out of the garage and left idle to warm up. "Yeah, old gal," said Elijah as he wiped the dust off, "We're going to try something different this weekend." Then he popped my hood and gave me a look-over, dipping fluids, admiring the precision of my mechanics.

We drove for well over an hour to a place called Morristown, outside The City, in Jersey. This was where Elijah and Eliza now lived. It's different out there. More space between people. Wide driveways. Quieter. More sky. And lots of grass. I was backed into the driveway and parked. I stayed overnight. The next morning, before daybreak, Elijah and Eliza loaded me with stuff I've never touched or seen before. Like a tent. Three large coolers. Gas stove. Sleeping bags. Food. Toilet paper.

Then others arrived. Elijah and Eliza's offspring, three of them, with their spouses and their kids. Three generations. And they added to my cargo. A football. Inflatable rafts. More toilet paper. More food. More coolers. After everyone had their fill, there was still room for more, and Arnold, the middle offspring, said he was impressed at how much I could swallow, and that I should have been used before. I remember I didn't understand what he meant by that. Used me *before*?

Elijah and I led the procession of family cars out of the city with his eldest grand-daughter, Amelia, riding shotgun. She and I get on well. Ever since she was a tiny kid. Elijah and Eliza often baby-sat at the funeral parlor. Amelia would always wander away to seek me. When she was real small, she liked to sneak inside my back, play with her dolls, and make house. When she got older, she was allowed to use me as her hangout, where she tapped the screen of her smart phone and pumped tunes through my eight-speaker sound system. She was the only one that ever really tested the power of that roar. One night, she got behind the wheel, started the car, quietly reversed out of the garage and we rolled around the neighborhood with Beyoncé booming.

I learned from Elijah and Amelia's conversation that we were driving to a place called Adirondacks. A many hour journey lay ahead. It felt good to build momentum, the fast rhythm of rolling tires, spinning gears to full wheel, flexing the pistons, get into stride at a speed of 65. I started to pay attention to the conversation inside when Amelia asked, "So, Grandpa, what's happening to Brunhilda?"

"Man-alive, Amelia, why you got to name the hearse that? I prefer Raquel."

"I've been calling her Brunhilda for years. You know that."

"What's a Broom Hilder? A German broom? I don't get it," Elijah said with a half-smile.

"Grandpa, this car is so Brunhilda."

"You keep saying that and it still makes me think of a bushy broom. This car is no bushy broom," said Elijah, and he patted my oak dash.

"Anyways, Grandpa, what's going to happen to Brunhilda?"

"Probably sell her. Don't think any of the other parlors want an old gal like this one, though."

"How about if I buy her?" asked Amelia.

"Why on Earth do you want a hearse?"

"Not just any hearse. It's Brunhilda," said Amelia. "You know how convenient it would be to drive to college? I can take just about all my stuff. I'd save on shipping and airfare. Brunhilda would make it to Oregon, easy. I've known her my entire life."

"Amelia! Come now! Brunhillier's too big. She goes through gas like nobody's business."

I never really thought about what was going to happen when the funeral parlor closed. I was caught in the routine of dutifully delivering the dead of Brooklyn. I figured I'd just work at another parlor, maybe as a reserve. Sure, in the back of my mind I knew death would eventually happen and, in the end, I'd get scrapped. I'm aware of how life works. But that was in the back of my mind. *Way, way* back.

What never entered my thoughts was a life outside The City. Something outside the dead. Amelia planted the seeds of these thoughts.

The family get-together was a camp. And it was in mountains. Adirondacks. Getting there involved my nose pointing upward and snaking over twisting roads. Smooth sailing. When we parked, everyone commented their surprise that I had no trouble keeping speed on mountain roads. Then they unloaded me. Waffle maker. Spare ribs. Tiki torches. Oars. Ax. Badminton set. All of it.

Amelia slept in the back. Before going to bed, she wrote in a journal, then read a book titled *Natural History of the Adirondacks*. She slept peacefully and, rested from my comforts, she awoke primed with energy. She arose before everyone else, and did yoga poses in the misty, early light, her long breaths fogging the exhale. Eliza awoke a few minutes later. She tried some of the yoga positions with her grand-daughter. Then both restarted the fire and made breakfast, the wooded air mixed with slices of fatty meat that sizzled in a fry pan over the fire.

During the day, there was a lot of lounging around. Amelia, though, always led some of the family away where cars couldn't go. After a few hours, they'd return sweaty, all happy, then head to the lake to cool down. At night, everyone circled around the campfire. I couldn't hear what they were talking about, but everyone was glowing.

After three days, everything was regathered, and each family made their own return. Amelia rode back with her mom and dad, while Eliza returned with Elijah. Elijah told her of Amelia's wish. Eliza objected with hew-hah about how a young woman shouldn't drive a car like me. Elijah, though, did start to warm up to the idea once we got closer to The City, and actually said, "The hearse could make it. There *and* back. No sweat, I don't doubt it."

Eliza, though responded with a heavy tone: "The car's too old."

And that was the last time I was let out for a run. Labor Day is around the corner. I'm just waiting, for what I don't know. Not for the dead. Perhaps waiting for my own demise. Perhaps my first long run to those Adirondacks was my last.

Although I have only 17,763 miles to my name, if I sit and think about it, I've witnessed a great change in The City. It's easy to miss change if you're busy in a routine. When I recall those first five years, in the 1980s, when I was real fresh, and compare them to now, it's a different world. There's less garlic in the air. The marshy rot of the East River dried and turned to promenades. The summers don't bake as hard. The winters are cleaner and hold less snow. Businesses that have been in the same family for generations make way for shiny cafes. The likes of Maurice Basi. When Maurice was twenty years younger but still an old man, Elijah and I saw him snap a radio antenna off a car with Jersey plates. Elijah laughed and said that Maurice must have needed a measuring stick to determine who's the bocce winner. But there are no old men playing bocce anymore, radio antennas are safe, I guess. Like everything else.

One thing I know that never changes, though, is *a hearse is given wide birth*. No one cuts me off. I don't get tailgaters. No one presses their horn. No one sneers. Everyone yields. Putting a scratch on a hearse must be some sort of curse. I mention this because it attests to my safety record. I'm the safest ride on the road. Perfect protection for a grand-daughter, right? When was the last time anyone talked about a hearse involved in an accident or a carjacking? Screw the dead. Give me your most precious.

What is Oregon? How far from Newark? Near Adirondacks? I get thinking about it and shivers run through my chassis. I've never broke down. I've seen regular maintenance, my belts top-notch. I know Amelia would have refined and pointed her argument further, pushed the issue more. She's a smart kid, and when she knows she's right she'll insist, not demure. Surely, Elijah will open the garage soon. And Amelia will be with him. And Elijah will unlock the driver door and just before taking the seat he will change his mind, stand, and give the keys to his grand-daughter, instructing her to start me up, reverse slowly, carefully. She would, too, negotiating the narrow exit with ease, her confidence contagious, and Elijah would know right there that this hearse, this gal, is the right fit.

OLD

PORTLAND

An out of town family looks at the café from the sidewalk. The father is working towards pot-bellied. Growing jowls. A Ring of Saturn remainder of hair orbiting his mass of baldness. Polo shirt tucked into his belted shorts. Loafers. White socks. The mother's a fusser. She could enjoy the vivid sunflower-print dress she's wearing, but instead, she's buzzing over her seven-year-old son, telling him to stop fidgeting, moving the fringe of his blonde hair away from his eyes. His older sister, a recent teenager, stands aloof, waits with headphones plugging her ears. The father approves the café and leads his family to its door.

As he's about to open the door, a bearded man in his twenties, wearing only boxer-briefs and a headband, triumphantly exits the café with a bulldog, a labradoodle, and a dachshund each reined to a master leash. The young man nods a good-day, salutes his coffee to the family, then walks away with his pack. The son points and a goofy, giant grin beams from his face. The mother slaps the boy's hand, but instead of pain he laughs and gestures that he wants to take his pants off. The teenage daughter is trying to take a photo of the dog-walker with her phone. The father moves his brood in the opposite direction, away from the café, to the food carts suggested by the travel guide book.

Eryn and Jasper watch from inside the café, standing behind the espresso machine. "Oh, don't go!" says Eryn, "I would have made the kids an awesome smoothie."

"I guess nothin'-but-underwear scares some," reasons Jasper.

"But he's walking around happy with three dogs who obviously adore him. That's not scary."

"It's weird, though."

"It's more sweet than weird. I like our regulars. They keep things interesting."

Jasper nods his head. "I'm with you. The half-dressed dog-walker always brings a smile to my face."

"Right?" affirms Eryn. "And what about Stavros. He's another that makes me smile."

Jasper prepares a fresh urn of drip coffee. "What *is* Stavros' story?"

"I think he has done a lot. Or at least seen a lot."

"But where's he from? Philippines? Morocco?"

"I don't know," she responds. "I always thought he's from Mexico, but that's just an assumption."

"And what does he do? He's always got cash in his wallet. It makes me think that he's a gambler or a loan shark."

Eryn shakes her head and furrows her eyes. "It's nothing glamorous like that. He's a landlord."

But Jasper pursues the line of thought. "And he drives around that old Cadillac. Have you seen how long that thing is? I think landlord is a front. He might be a pimp!" He laughs at his assumptions.

"Whatever," says Eryn. "He's interesting. I closed Sunday and he kept me company. He told a story about his last visit to New York and hooking-up with an ice-skater who had a third nipple."

"Wow," says Jasper. "Yeah, I bet he has no problems with the ladies."

Eryn moves to the food prep area. "No, it wasn't crass. There was more to it. Much more. He sets scenes, goes into details, delivers it with humor. You know how slow closing can be. It's fun when he hangs out and decides to chat. It beats leaning against the espresso machine looking at the clock."

"I wish he'd kick it with me," admits Jasper. "I'd really like to hear a kink story about three nipples. I should try to strike up a conversation with him. Maybe about music. Hey, do you mind if I put my tunes on?"

Blondie is playing in the background. "Sure," says Eryn. "But that means you have to make the food orders."

Jasper unplugs Eryn's phone and connects his to the house stereo. A contemporary RnB song with wandering female vocals, auto-tuned, and a heavy bass drum floods the speakers. "This is DJ Klue's remix of Beyoncé," announces Jasper, with a raised voice. "Man, that beat has got some serious backbone!" Jasper sings along a few bars in falsetto, neck-snaps back and forth to the rhythm.

Eryn retrieves her phone and lowers Jasper's volume a little. He doesn't notice the lowered volume but soon notices Eryn is no longer talking. She is staring blankly towards the door. "So, what's the story about the third nipple?" asks Jasper.

Eryn turns to him. "There's no way I can recount it as good as Stavros. I'm not as funny. You should ask him to tell you."

Jasper considers. "Ha! That's weird. I mean, you know, giving him change for his coffee and then casually dropping, 'Hey, Eryn says you should tell me the story about the gal with the extra nipple.'"

Eryn smirks. "Sure, you should do it just like that. You're going to need a good ten minutes of free time, though. It's a story that shouldn't be rushed."

The café doors open. A mechanic from the auto repair store a block away enters and nods at Jasper.

"Hi," says Jasper. "How are you?"

"Alright," says the mechanic. "I'll just get a large coffee to go."

"That's three dollars."

As the mechanic leaves with coffee in hand, Jasper continues. "What is the lead-up to a three-nipple story, anyways?"

"We were talking about getting old, how the body and mind slip. Then Stavros says, 'Suicide is never off the table, Eryn.' I mean, wow, who says things like that?"

"Whoa! He's suicidal?"

"No, he says he's not. It's just an option always available. Anyways, I quoted a line by Spinoza that has always stuck with me." Eryn pauses and searches for the words. "*A free man thinks of nothing less than of death and his wisdom is a meditation not on death but on life.* I repeated that line when Stavros mentioned suicide. He smiled, thought about it, then recounted the New York story with the ice skater."

Jasper rakes his scrappy beard. "That sounds like a wild tangent."

"More like a nice tangent. It was his way of telling me that he gets what Spinoza is talking about."

"Cool, cool," says Jasper. "Has Lewis met him? Sounds like they would get along."

"No, not yet. He'll probably meet Lewis when he picks me up for the date."

Jasper freezes. "Date? Say what now?"

A carpenter enters the café, wearing overalls, a flat pencil behind his ear, a steel ring pierced through his nose, a silver-capped front tooth, salt-and-pepper billy-goat beard running down to his Adam's Apple, and around his neck a wooden rosary. He approaches the counter.

"Hi, Tad," says Eryn. "Just the coffee?"

"Ahoy hoy," replies Tad, and he places down a dollar seventy-five in quarters. "How are you?"

"Good."

"Did you see what's hangin' from the power lines out front?" asks Tad.

"A pair of shoes?"

"No."

"I give up. What?"

Tad pumps coffee from the self-serve urn into his cup. He smiles wide, his silver-capped tooth glints. "You need to go and look yourself. It's something to be experienced not spoken. Trust me not!" And with that, he exits through the back door to the patio smoking section.

Eryn and Jasper go outside and hanging from the power lines are a pair of dildos, flesh colored, tied together with shoelace. Like nunchucks. Eryn and Jasper turn to each other, laugh, and re-enter the café.

"Dicks in the sky," jokes Eryn. "Dongs on a wire!"

Jasper joins in. "Dildo tight-rope!"

"I wonder if it's the result of a break-up?" queries Eryn with a mischievous smile. "Like, the ex stole the dildos and lobbed them up for everyone to see."

"Let that be a lesson," proclaims Jasper. "Hide your sex toys before breaking up."

Two people enter and order bagels. Then another arrives and orders a tuna melt. Jasper makes them faster than usual, then, while nonchalantly cleaning the counter, he asks, "So, you and Lewis are having problems?"

Eryn flatly answers. "Uh, no."

"Oh..." Jasper furrows his eyebrows, rubs the counter top with more elbow grease, as if a beet stain is sinking deeper.

"I like Stavros but it's not like that," says Eryn. "He's really interesting. He's picking me up in his old Cadillac and taking me to a fancy restaurant that has valet parking. How often does that happen to you?"

"It's really none of my business," says Jasper, and he looks at other places that need a wipe.

"No, it's cool, you're not prying." She acknowledges, "I'm the one that brought up the subject."

Jasper throws the wipe rag into the laundry hamper and props himself against the fridge. "Wow... And Lewis knows?"

"Of course he knows!"

"Wow. Sorry, I mean..."

Eryn laughs.

Jasper blushes, but then he laughs, too. "I'm sorry," he says. Then, "You know, I'm just picturing Stavros knocking on the door of your house, dressed in a suit, with flowers. Here's a guy that might be old enough to be your dad, and he's going to meet the man of the house, your boyfriend, before taking you out on a date. That's a mixed-up role reversal."

"Ha!" Eryn exclaims with a smile and nod. "Yeah, that's not common. I don't think I am leading Stavros on. I hope not." She peers outside, looks for distance. "No, I'm not. He invited Lewis as well, but I said that's cool, we're just going out as friends. He needs friends, I think. He's lonely."

Jasper nods. "I wonder how old is he, anyway?"

"I don't know," says Eryn. "He was joking about killing himself when he turns 50."

"So, he's younger than 50. Maybe close?" queries Jasper.

"He's probably 56," answers Eryn.

They both laugh.

"You're right, though," Jasper admits. "I'd go to dinner with him if he asked me. A steak dinner."

Eryn looks at the clock. "I'm going to take lunch now, if that's cool."

Jasper surveys the tables, the only people inside are two activists nursing coffees. "Sure. Whatcha having? I'll make it for you."

"That's sweet. But I'm just going to grab a bagel."

"How about a little bacon, sliced tomato..."

"No, I got my own tomato," and from her bag Eryn fishes out a large heirloom variety.

"Holy shit!" exclaims Jasper. "That's a tomato."

"Yes. Yes it is," says Eryn in deadpan. She then fumbles around in her bag and finds another. "Here, you can have this. I grew it myself."

"You grew it?"

"Yes." Eryn looks at Jasper with a serious face. "I am

the Tomato Bandit of North Portland."

A July night, five years ago, Eryn and Lewis moved a futon to the front porch to claim the cool evening breeze. They were both listening to the crickets chirp when they heard a rustle in their front yard. It was their neighbor from across the street, an old lady with crooked back, on her knees digging. They quietly watched, unnoticed, as the old lady planted two tomato seedlings. After finishing their yard, she shuffled to the next and planted again. She embedded the entire block before returning home. Her house was a small cottage, with a worn dandelion pocked lawn, and rows of container plants where tin cans, buckets, and a pedestal sink were re-purposed into pots.

Most of the old lady's guerrilla tomatoes didn't last. One or two maintained, if in reach of automatic sprinklers. Eryn and Lewis watered and feed theirs, nurturing them to large vines bearing fat fruit. The old lady noticed. Every time she saw either Eryn or Lewis, she waved and smiled with a little laugh of joy. The old lady maintained her replant enterprise the next two years. But one winter, she was stretchered to an ambulance. Her house was sold, demolished, and replaced with a three story whose footprint claimed most of the property, leaving room only for a small flower-bed and thin strip of fresh lawn. That summer, though, tomatoes reappeared in the neighborhood with vengeance, not only on the block but in the surrounding blocks, including a thriving Roma next to the convenience store. In the small flower-bed across the street, the new home owners discovered a young heirloom and watered the plant, which rewarded them with fruit the size of fists. The following year, they replaced the lawn with a planter box and grew more, as well as pole beans and kale.

TRAMPO MARX LAUNCHES INTO SPACE

In the time before the rocket, I adapted a routine, waking early to watch the sun bubbling up from Gulf of Mex, standing on top of sand dune and welcoming dawn with appreciative eyes like the blue heron. Satisfied with the sun, I walk back behind the dunes, inland a hundred yards or so into scrubbery plain, to the leeward side of a rocky outcrop, where at my camp I boil coffee and warm corn tortillas, buttering them to make Mexican toast and maybe sneak some leftover fish. After breakfast, I mosey to the beach, wash coffee mug in sea, and I too, give myself a bathe, disrobe right there 'cause no one's around. I dunk under surf, remain submerged until lungs yell what gives, then spring out like a happy porpoise, inhaling great gasp of ocean air.

I'm not keen with precise accounting of time. Sun arrives and departs, moon tugs and pushes sea, that's all I needs to know. I never understood waking to beeping alarm clock, starting the day with begrudged, sleepy eyes and weight of forebode. It never worked that way for me and I think I'm better for it. Myself, I begin the day in peace and I bet I've got a better heart-beat than anyone half my age. Fit as a knee-slapper dancin' fiddle-player, as they say in Appalachia.

Some time ago, I left the industrial heart of the North East with a shopping cart loaded only with necessities. The plan was to roll 'round the continental states but once I got here to the cut-lip of Texas, where the Rio Grande whimpers beat into the ol' Gulf of Mex, I looked ahead and saw desert wretchedness and chip-toothed mountains that filled me with great apprehension. While where I was standing, toes wiggling in lapping waters and silvery beach, was a place that provided sustenance year-round and a kind climate that doesn't freeze nor lack rain. I decided to Goldilocks it and make myself at home instead of rolling on.

This place is called Boca Chica. A straight translate from Spanish into English is Mouth Girl but the connotation is the mouth is small, and that's how the Rio Grande finishes, a somber, wade-able exit slipping into the yawn of Gulf. It's a far cry from its headwaters high in the Colorado Rocks, where the muscles of snow pack and glacier melt careens the river fresh through New Mexico, then elbows east at El Paso, even regains haste through canyons on the Mexas border but then suffers great drains of irrigation on both sides of border until it, like I said, whimpers beat into The Gulf.

I arrived at Boca Chica just after parting ways with a traveling buddy, a smart mutt named Hot Cheese. He joined me in Louisiana. He was a young stray and when he saw my shopping-cart down the streets of Baton Rogue he figured a better life with me. We traversed Louisiana and got through most of Texas but then the law befell upon us in South Padre Island. I made the wrong decision to camp there and should have known better. High rise condos and schmancy hotels, boulevards lined with sports-bars and tourist junkets, are indications that the scene won't take too kindly to the likes of me and Hot Cheese. I thought I was crafty and camped far from the condo end of the isle, a good mile from the commotion. But The Fuzz found us after one night. It was morning, I was brewing coffee on the Sterno, Hot Cheese was chewing jerky, when the law wheeled in, big no-neck fellas, didn't even say howdy, and gave me the choice of going back over the bridge to the mainland or spend downtime in lockup. I said, "No argument from me, officers," and I packed camp fast into the shopping cart. I was just about ready to roll out but the authorities wanted to tangle more and made inquiries about Hot Cheese – where's his license, his rabies shot, proof of ownership. They didn't really want to listen to my answers, and they adjudicated that the dog be confiscated. They led Hot Cheese away to the cruiser and the dog morosely went but at the last second he quickly jolted clean from gripped collar and sprinted into the dunes with tubby, no-neck popo chasing pathetically for a few yards before giving up.

I waited on the other side of the bridge just outside city limits, even camped in a ditch overnight, holding out for Hot Cheese but he didn't show. And that was that, our paths diverted, nothing to do but wish for the best and push down the road to see what's next.

Which was Boca Chica. Hot Cheese would have loved it here. The road to Boca Chica is a long, flat single lane stretching 20 lonely miles from the outskirts of Brownsville. The nearest building is the US Border Patrol checkpoint, which consists of a hut, a portapotty, and crossing arm that's left raised. When I first rolled in, the lone border guard was waiting outside his station. He seen me rolling from miles away through binoculars, didn't believe his eyes until I'm there before him. Not many cars come this way, they're usually on the other side of the shipping channel, heading to the curated beach of South Padre Island. A shopping cart tramp in these parts is rare. I tipped my hat. Border guard gave a hello sir, noticed the fishing poles and net on the side of my cart and says, "Good fishing out there, near the mouth, the river's full of nutrients. Fish come from all around to feed in the waters."

I thanked him kindly for the advice and he held out his hand for a shake and introduced himself. "My name's Carl," he said. "When the road ends at the beach, turn right, and a couple of miles or so is the best fishing. Where the fresh and salt water meet. You'll see the pelicans dive. Cast there and get yourself a surf fish."

And Carl was right. I fish every day, fish is my number one protein, my lunch and dinner only costs time and effort but I tells ya, I don't think of fishing in terms of cost nor survival. I like to wade out at low tide, follow the back of a sand bar a hundred yards from the shore and when the lumbering swells get high on my chest and I don't dare go further, I hurl my line as far as I can. I like to look back at the fading land, reminding myself how little I am. If I am here or not, the scene carries on. I am grateful to be here. I'd stay out longer, where the only sound is water and air, but the fish are greedy and gobble the hook, Spanish Mackerel, eight to ten pounders, real torpedoes streaked with florescent greens and blues. I don't like catching more than I can eat – one Spanish Mack is plenty – and if I stay out there with a catch in my basket and recast I am inviting a fish I don't need, as well as the attention of dog sharks that have no trouble taking a chomp of submerged legs.

It was a few days after I arrived when I got two Spanish Macks, big fellas, the second swallowed the barb deep and I couldn't detach and release, so I was trudging back to camp with these two fish hooked and dangling dead from my belt when I sees a family on the Mexican side of the Rio Grande setting up camp. Two boys ditched supposed chores and charged into the river, dashed across to the American side, then chased each other back and forth. They were laughing as they splashed from shore to shore, and whenever they got to the American side, their guffaws grew to out-of-breath jocularity. The rest of their family were setting up for a day at the beach, stringing tarps, grandma, mother, and toddler daughter setting up cocina on the truck flatbed. Hitched to the truck on its own trailer rested a BBQ, a 70-gallon metal barrel cut in half and hinged open, the father of the clan filling it with wood chunks.

As I approached, the two boys saw me, ran to the Mexican side, waved and yelled something in Spanish. I figured they were doing their buenas días because, damn, it sure was a beautiful day and I remember being young and over-exuberant, so I waved a howdy-do back. By the time I reach the river their father had come down from the BBQ and joined his sons. The father nodded at me and I mirrored likewise.

"Good looking fish, man," he says over the river. "Mackerel, eh?"

"Yes-sir," I's say, and move to the river edge. We chat and he gets to talking about his father-in-law who used to

93

fish here and deep sea, too, around the oil rig pylons where the sea bass frolic. I tell him where I get my Mack, about the sunken sandbar that only presents itself at low tide. We chin-wag like that for awhiles, his kids run away and resume counting-coo with the border. They have a strong grasp of geography, these children.

I liked the story of his Father-In-Law. He told it as if mentioning him was an honor. I looked at my catch and handed him the bigger one.

"Oh, man, I can't take your fish."

"Brother-man, you'd be doing me a favor, I don't need two fish, I ain't got no refridge or ice, it's either you take this and get old ma to make a nice dish or it goes to the gulls."

He paused a little, debated within himself, then took the fish and held it in his arm like a football. He then offered his hand for a shake. "Gracias. My name is Salvo."

Salvo and his familia appeared the following week, too. I was heading out to the sand bar when Salvo saw me, waved, and ran down to the river. "Thanks for the fish, man," he said. "Abuela loved it."

"No problem, friend."

"You going out to fish?"

I nodded.

"Say, how about you catch a couple extra and bring them up here and we'll smoke some. I'm cooking cabrito... We'll swap meats. You should eat with us."

Very kind, I said, and accepted, figuring it was the neighborly thing to do, a good way to build international relations. And I like baby goat. So I went out to the sand bank, cast and scored two long Spanish Macks. Fifteen minutes later, I was wading across the Rio Grande holding the Macks high like super-trophies and Salvo waved rejoice, and met me in the river with a big smile and lightened my load. It had been some time since I visited Mexico.

They were genuine to me from the beginning, even abuela, who I bet is generally suspicious of everyone but liked me from the get go, appreciates a man who can take care of himself. She smiled and nodded and thanked for the fish, I make out that it's her favorite, and she reaches for the fish to clean them and, when I realized that she was going to do the dirty job of de-gut, I insisted that I do it. This made me a gentleman in her eyes.

And they grilled cabrito, butterfly split and speared on a stick that was angled over the coals. Sweating in a cast iron on the side were a pot of beans. Little daughter made the pico de gallo. And they set me up with a mighty lump of masa to make corn tortillas back at my camp. A big bag of dough to make, what Salvo described as chingos of tortillas. Abuela pan-fried Mack fillets in manteca, cornflour breaded, then vegetated with a crop of cilantro and made tacos and man, they showed me how to cook simple and eat good.

They set tents after dinner and built a campfire, where we gentlemen retire to digest.

"Here, friend," Salvo says and hands me a beer.

"Gracias but I don't drink alcohol. I used to and it didn't work out too well," I says.

"It's all good, I understand, it's important to keep your head," he says and cracks open his tallboy and sits on the beach chair and we watch the sunset with our backs towards the sun, as the waves and clouds and seagulls and seaweed, all of it, goes subdued in the falling light. "Sure is beautiful," says Salvo, turning his eyes to his kids making sand castles around their mother as she reads a magazine. Salvo then fishes out a joint from his shirt pocket and lights it.

"Now, that," I says nodding to the joint, "is something I do well with," and Salvo laughs, passes it to me and it was just ordinary Mexican brick weed but it burnt good and puff puff, I am stoned, and the waves and clouds and seagulls, all of it, continue to slow dance in the going day, and I think a quiet thanks.

I asks, "What do you do, Salvo? How do you make your money?"

"I'm a welder. A good one, too. There's always work for a welder, everywhere. Good pay."

"Is that so?"

"Oh yes. I've worked all the way up the west coast, from Alaskan pipeline down to Acapulco. At the moment, I'm working near where you are camped."

"Out in the shipping channel?"

"No, near you...."

He could see that I didn't know what he was talking about.

"The launch pad. You know, for the rocket ship."

Maybe the beer and mota made Salvo say the oddest things but he was insistent and told me to look for the entrance off Boca Chica Road about a mile before it ends at the beach.

The next day, I hiked to where Salvo said there was the rocket launch pad. Indeed, there was a gravel road leading half mile into the flood plains where a large expanse was restricted by a chain-link fence. I was expecting more and wouldn't have noticed it if I wasn't told. I followed the gravel, got to the fence, and patrolled the perimeter for a mile or so until I could make out in the middle of the compound a large concrete oval, a scatter of pre-fab buildings and a parked bulldozer. I was expecting Space Age. I had a picture in mind – a standing rocket piping steam, gnats of gizmos, security, big booms of spotlights, landing lights blinking, buildings of computers and engineers, and burly security with machine-gunned jeeps declaring keep back without speaking. But it wasn't anything of the sort. More like a mall car park for a mall that never got built.

I walked back to the road and wandered to the border check-point. After polite greets and exchange of how doings, I asks Carl the border guard, "Is that really a launch pad near the beach?"

"Yes, sir," he says. "Space X, it's called."

"Sounds like a 1950's sci-fi movie," I says. "What kind of rocket they gonna launch from out here?"

"Satellites into orbit. Running supplies to the space station. It's a private company, not NASA."

"Sweet Jesus, it don't look like much."

"The age of computers. Press a button in New York, launch a rocket on the Gulf coast. Some guy who made a bunch of money on the Internet is now interested in the space ship business."

"I guess a man needs to occupy his time with what brings happiness," I says. "I like fishing. Another guy likes to play Star Trek. I just can't imagine a rocket ship shooting from here. Where is the tower, you know, some sort of control tower?"

"Beats me, I'm no engineer," says Carl. "They say they're going to do a test launch end of next month. A sounding rocket."

When Salvo and his fam came to their side of the

river the following weekend, I told them of the upcoming launch. Salvo got excited. "Cool, man," he said. "I'm going to bring the kids, take them out of school. That's a firework, *cabrón*, with an education."

I could see Salvo's point that brought him inquisitive joy but I was touched with a sense of unease, 'cause maybe I was getting squeezed out from here, too. In the weeks that followed, I put such worry in the back barn of my brain and remained busy, explored more, especially up-river where lost limbs of Rio Grande turned swamp and downright Jurassic, with old fat palm trees grouped around muddy mosquito lagoons and humidity slathering thick. Walking back from there one late afternoon I saw an ocelot with a lizard in its mouth and once it saw me it ran fast into the hiddens of the swamp. Funny ocelot... If you're scared of little me, I thought, then how's your bones gonna rattle when that rocket lights up.

I made improvements at the camp. An empty plastic ballast drum that fell off a cargo ship washed in. I commandeered, propped it up against the boulder outcrop of my camp, fashioned channels to funnel water and presto, I got myself a rain collector. Fresh water is needed more for coffee and thirst. Constant baths of salt water is no good, the salt dries on the skin. Important to sponge down before bed otherwise I'll be an itching sonovabitch all night.

After telling Salvo the fortune of my rain collector, he said I should start growing food, and he and his boys came out to my camp the following week with tomato and lettuce seeds, lugging big bags of potting soil over the river. They were impressed with my setup and saw it for what it is: shanty on the junkside, but ordered and clean.

I visited the launch pad again. I climbed the fence and walked to the paved middle. Various geometric shapes and numbers were freshly painted. I looked from the center and there was no vegetation to shake, no geography to hinder the sharp sun. From my pocket I pulled out a rock and scratched my presence on the launch pad: *Trampo Marx, Earth*. Later that night, back at camp, I untarped the shopping cart and oiled its wheels.

Then the day of the launch arrived. In the morning, security dudes wearing polo shirts on lousy ATVs drove down the beach on the American side to clear any people. They didn't see me or the camp, just peed on a sand dune, drank their Gatorade, and got back on their cursed vehicles and out of here. I was prepared to make a dash to Mexico if it came to it.

Salvo and familia arrived midday. Ol' sun was gracious, letting clouds bandy beneath it, the waves humble, and present was the ideal breeze running at the right moments to cool overheat. Although the children were not at school, they were required to do all of the work and set up camp and grill barrel under abuela's supervision while Salvo and missus went for a long hand-in-hand walk down the beach. After finishing chores, the boys went for a splash while baby sister played sand castles, then the boys joined in and made a moat saying that the princess and her castle needed protection and as brothers who better.

I arrived with my hand-made spear slung on my shoulder. The boys were keen to hold it, asked why it was so solid. "Used to be an arm of a mesquite," I says, "one of the hardest of hardwoods." I told them I was going to hunt stingray for dinner, and they laughed, thought I was joking, and I said, "No, in fancy restaurants they call it skate and rich folks pay high end for it." The boys followed me into the shallows. I told them to tread light, not stir the mud and keep an eye out. I came across a stingray, well camouflaged with a spread of sand on its back, and I walked past it a little until the boys were right next. They didn't see and I told them to stop and stand still, then I pointed next to their feet and as they backed-up surprised, stingray fled, rippled away into deeper water. The boys were aghast but then laughed. Now they knew.

We walked further and I spied another. I gestured to pause then quickly speared before the boys lost their statue, whip went the stingray tail and its barb sprung. I hoisted it out and away, then walked onto shore with boys cheering. They rubbernecked as I carved and skinned the wings, revealing pearly flesh. They wanted the barb, but I put it in the fire. They watched it burn. For dinner we had surf and turf: Skate and fajita tacos.

As the sun began to set, we all gathered at the beach with blankets and lounge chairs, looking back into the good ol' USA, waiting. When the skies started to lose peach, a rumble marshaled, then like a sizzling zipper going up, a skinny rocket defying gravity. It didn't look like it was ever going to stop but zipper all the way to the toe-nail moon. Following it, a long tail of vapor changing colors from purple to red to gold. And the rasp of the engine, the afterburner, like a short blade of sun. The family oohed and ahhed. I did, too, but with some regret because the Milky Way and rolling surf were always impressive enough.

HOW TO BOOGIE IN NEW ORLEANS

The first thing he does is make sure the phone is off. Not in sleep mode. Off. Completely. Notifications kill stealth. Without stealth, he's just like everybody else. He doesn't want to be mapped or located, leave a record of presence. The Find My Phone setting is ridiculous to him. He'd rather lose the phone.

He has never been caught.

His name is Cornelius, although one of Cornelius' favorite sayings is *never offer your real name 'cause it only gets in the way*. He's on the descending side of middle-aged. Time has been kind. Give him a shave, put him in a suit with a crisp open-collar shirt, and he's a silver fox. Cornelius, however, prefers the low-key comfort of jeans and sweats.

It's past midnight. Overcast. The spill of freeway lights flush the clouds dirty orange. No breeze. The air wants to stick. When it was liquid, some of the humidity was hot dog water.

It's the back-end of the French Quarter near Marigny. Cornelius is wearing a black track suit and he's on the roof of a three-story row house.

If the commercial and tourist trade now dictates the streets of the Quarter, the roofs are the last of old New Orleans. Generations of paint peeling from hand-milled woodwork, layers of shingles and tar, slipshod repairs, spits of glue and caulk, the roof line neither linear nor uniform from one building to the next, instead a jumble of interconnected peaks, slopes, and valleys.

And skylights. The skylight is the next best thing to a front door key. Old or new, it really doesn't matter, although Cornelius favors the new ones. Wired with an alarm, too. Such a skylight is not a deterrent, it's a tell. It says something valuable is inside.

Crouching to maintain a low center of gravity, Cornelius is keeping an eye out for access points while nimble-toeing from one roof to the next. His curiosity is piqued by an old stained-glass skylight. It's unwashed and opaque from years of city exhaust but with patient eyes the shape and pattern of a fanned peacock appears.

He surveys the building. The front half facing the street holds a PR firm on the ground floor, and two stories of condos above it. The skylight belongs to the back half of the building – a three-story home. Ivy chokes the wrought iron railing on the upper floor veranda. The ground floor is a garage and an entrance opening to an alley. No light slips from any windows.

Cornelius clears a spot on the skylight and spies the inside. The room below is used for storage. Boxes stacked, and furniture draped. The wallpaper has lost luster. Cornelius observes for ten minutes, detects no sign of movement, then opens the skylight with a bent stretch of wire and shimmy bar. He drops silently into the room. The air inside is older. Cornelius maintains his landing like a gymnast ending a parallel bars routine.

He hop-skips to a wall, creeps to the closed door, presses an ear to it, and remains there until his ear begins to sweat. Nothing. He turns the door handle, with slow precision, safe-cracker like, and opens the door in an even slower manner to prevent creaking getting any louder than a sleepy murmur.

A hallway. And the top of a staircase. Some of the wallpaper is unglued and flopping over itself. Carpeting. Once plush and bright with pattern. Now, like everything, shadowed by dust. Cornelius resumes his slow steps towards an ajar door. A bathroom. Unused for some time, a rust stained sink and claw-foot bath tub collecting dead moths and cockroaches. The next room's door is open. Another bedroom. Smaller, with a single bed. A guest room, no personal items. At the end of the hallway, a closed door. Cornelius again presses his ear against it and holds it there. Nothing. After opening the door in slow motion, he finds the master bedroom. Very ordered but dust given carte blanche. Chandelier and sconce lighting. Antique furniture. A four-post queen-sized bed. Undisturbed linen with sharp corners. There is a pocket watch, cuff-links, a tie pin, and a few hundred dollars on the dresser. Cornelius leaves them, for the time being.

Cornelius won't steal just anything. It's nothing to do with resale value or taste. Rather there's a righteousness with his acquisitions. Providence is key. If a high-carat diamond ring, passed from generation to generation with tales of smitten love presents itself during a burglary, Cornelius won't steal that ring no matter how big the sparkle. But if that same ring is inside a condo that belongs to an oil executive who purchased it from Sotheby's as a present for his mistress – bingo, that ring is a long-gone daddy.

On the second floor, Cornelius walks through the kitchen. Dead plants on a window sill. A fruit bowl that once held something. A loaf of bread turned to brick. A refrigerator that doesn't look inviting, more like a disinterred coffin. The air is less dank, though. A draft infiltrates under a swing door. A soft light accompanies it. Cornelius hears a window air-conditioner unit switch on. A more pronounced draft shifts the door slightly open. He stares at the peeking light and maintains a staring contest for ten minutes. The light never blinks; no shadow breaks it.

Opening the door, there's a dining table, old mahogany, ringed by high-backed chairs. Running along the length of a wall is a sideboard with a triumph of tarnished silverware. Stretching above it, an ornately framed but cloudy mirror reflecting light from the adjoining parlor.

In the parlor, a single bulb from a lampshade, and next to the lampshade, someone sits in a leather recliner, back turned, with only the top of a head visible. It appears a poorly fitted wig rests on the head.

Cornelius freezes, as if freezing renders him invisible.

The air-conditioning clicks off.

Cornelius listens for five minutes and only hears his breathing. He then breaks his freeze and casually walks into the parlor.

The person sitting beside the lampshade is dead. Dead for a long time. The dead is wearing a red smoking jacket over a waistcoat and an ascot. A book sits on the dead's lap: Ayn Rand's *Atlas Shrugged*.

It's not a wig. Just a dead comb over on a dehydrated

head. The corpse is mummified and well preserved, as if the skin went through a tannery. There is no smell of rot. Hanging onto the face are half-moon spectacles. Arms are balanced on each arm rest. The recliner's is extended but the dead's left foot has fallen to the floor, detached at the ankle where the tendon decayed and skin thinned too much.

Cornelius sits opposite in the matching recliner and takes a hard look. Died with mouth wide open. Cornelius has never been with a corpse outside a funeral home, but he doesn't show any surprise. Surprise is losing cool and control.

Look at that mouth, thinks Cornelius. The dropped bottom jaw pulled by tightening skin, exaggerating an overbite. It reminds Cornelius that he, when sleeping, is a mouth breather. A snorer. Cornelius thinks about dying in his sleep, his mouth overhung, airway struggling. He mirrors the corpse's profile to see how it feels.

Cornelius is single. His last affair was with a young lady twenty-five years his junior. An English Literature grad. She insisted he sleep with a mouth-piece designed to cut snoring. He did, and she still left him.

Cornelius has no children. No siblings. He has an aunt who drools in a Florida nursing home.

Cornelius' closest friend is his fence, Maurice. Technically, Maurice is a fence of a fence. Although Maurice has fenced for Cornelius close to three decades, and they've shared a few late-night revelries and drinks, Cornelius has never met Maurice's wife or sons, or stepped inside Maurice's house.

In Cornelius' hard look at the dead in the recliner, he reflects a likely future. His profession's discretion and secrecy has come at a cost. He, too, could die like Smoking Jacket and no one would know. Cornelius thinks how weird it would be to be struck by a heart attack at this very instant. Two forgotten corpses.

"You look thirsty," says Cornelius, and acknowledges the bar in the corner of the parlor. "I think we need to get ourselves a drink."

The bar is also old mahogany, maybe the same tree as the dining table, with carvings of a wandering vine rolling around its front. Behind the bar, an impressive stock of liquor, heavy with cognac and single malt scotch. Cornelius picks a bottle and reads the label aloud. "Gleg-gorang-whda-nal. Wedy-nal. Gleg-gorhend-wed-nal. Gleg-gablah-blah-blah." He turns to the corpse. "My, my, friend. I can't pronounce it, but I bet this eighteen-year-old liquor has aged another fifty in this here bottle. Am I right?" Cornelius pulls drawer handles and finds a bar towel. He whips the dust off the bar, blows clean two brandy snifters, then pours generously.

He returns to the corpse. "Here, let's get that gone," and Cornelius removes the book from the dead lap and places it on the side table, the back-cover photo of Ayn Rand facing up. Cornelius places the corpse's glass on top of it.

Cornelius sits in his recliner, rolls the whiskey around his glass, and pokes his nose into it. "Hot damn," he says and takes a deeper inhale before pulling the glass away, his eyes stung red. Raising the whiskey to the lamp, he admires the hue. Cornelius announces, "Yes sir, this here is Scotland!" After savoring a small sip, then another longer one, he sinks deep into the recliner.

There is an inherent sadness of dying unnoticed.

Cornelius ponders this. It usually means that the life was unnoticed, too. Alone. If a tree falls on a desert island. Dead before you're dead. What kind of life is that? More isolation than life.

Cornelius searches the room for distraction from these glum thoughts. Bookshelves filled. Wood paneling. Oil paintings of antebellum romance. At the end of the room a pair of closed pocket doors. Cornelius stands, walks over, and slides the doors open.

"Jay-sus, Mister."

A billiard table awaits. Switching on the overhead spotlights, the vibrancy of the felt verdants the room. He racks the balls, then goes back to the bar and refills with a different bottle of scotch. As he pours he sees the stereo. He dials the volume knob to zero before turning it on, then raises the volume slowly. It's already tuned to a jazz station. "I like yours taste," Cornelius says over his shoulder to the corpse. He dances back to the billiard table with the glass in one hand and bottle in the other.

"Straight pool, dollar a ball. Any objections?"

Cornelius sharpens the pool stick with chalk, lines up for the break, pulls the stick back and forth in rhythm to the music then drills the cue ball. A puff of blue follows the shot. A ball falls in a pocket.

"Before I continue," says Cornelius as he decants more liquor into his glass, "a toast to yours hospitality. You got fine digs." He raises his glass, tips his head, and sinks the scotch in one gulp.

Cornelius plays pool for an hour, sometimes pauses his game and dances with the cue if the radio strikes the right tune. He starts practicing trick shots, pushing spin on the cue ball to increase angles and reverse potential but the drink slowly turns his game sour. Cornelius retires to his recliner with bottle and glass.

"Man, that's a gorgeous table." He attempts to recharge his glass but discovers the bottle is empty. "Say, looks like you ain't drinking," and Cornelius takes the corpse's glass sitting on Ayn Rand's face, then nestles into the recliner, extending the leg rest.

Books line the shelves; shelves coil the room. Pottery and framed photos intermittently interrupt the book procession. The photo nearest to Cornelius shows a flaring peacock in front of someone sitting in a rickshaw, smiling at the camera. The color in the photo was made in the 1960s.

On the side of the bar, there's a bull-whip hanging from a hook. A fez and a matador hat roost on a stand.

In the far corner, in a small alcove, is a shrine consisting of a crucifix, a statue of a five-headed elephant, spent incense, and an old, well-thumbed gris-gris.

"You know, and I bet you agree," says Cornelius to the corpse, "the best way to die is in your own bed, with wife and children and grand childs standing around you, looking down with teary eyes but also, at the same time, smiling. Tears 'cause goodbye's sad. Smiles 'cause they're thankful and proud that you were in their life. That's honor and respect and love. Imagine that as your last earthly feeling. The very last! That's the best way to go. No doubt."

The air-conditioning switches on. The radio announcer is talking about Miles Davis' second great quintet.

"Not everyone dies like that," acknowledges Cornelius. "Some die far worse. Sitting on the can. Or lying in a gutter. Gunshot to the gut. Thrown down a well. Buried alive. Like them folks in Pompeii. That's a tough deal, man.

That's *far* from the ideal.

"But friend, look at you!" Cornelius waves his arms around the room, the remainder of whiskey flung from the snifter. "You died a good life. There's satisfaction in that. Could be worse. Far worse."

Cornelius folds his recliner and stands. He expresses solemn appreciation to the host and bows near a right-angle. While facing the floor, Cornelius rediscovers the corpse's felled foot. He picks it up, attempts to re-perch it to the ankle but the foot finds no balance and falls. Cornelius tries again, this time engineering *Atlas Shrugged* and the empty scotch bottle as bookends, bracing the foot in between. It successfully stands. Satisfied that it will persist, Cornelius lets himself out.

CPSIA information can be obtained
at www.ICGtesting.com
Printed in the USA
LVHW090814211019
634812LV00004B/472/P

9 781732 391031